I0587531

CALL OF THE SEA

CALL OF THE LYCAN

MICHELLE M. PILLOW

MICHELLE M. PILLOW® - MICHELLEPILLOW.COM

Call of Sea (Call of the Lycan) © Copyright 2006 - 2018, Michelle M. Pillow

Second Print Edition July 2018

First Print Edition September 25, 2017

Second Electronic Printing April 2011

First Electronic Printing July 2006

Published by The Raven Books LLC

ISBN 978-1-62501-192-3

ABOUT CALL OF THE SEA

PARANORMAL SHIFTER ROMANCE

Werewolf Ian O'Connell, heir prince to his clan, has no plans to settle down even though his untamed nature keeps him on the prowl for female company. The only woman he could ever want saved him from a watery grave before disappearing from his life forever. But that was a long time ago, too long for a mortal woman to have survived. Though he searched for her, in the end it was in vain.

Cursed by the power of the Cancerian crab, Ceana is doomed to spend her eternity in the ocean as a mermaid. Her only relief is on a full moon, when she becomes human and must find shore. Centuries have passed and she's all but given up on the one who could save her. Brief passion is all she has and she's willing to take what she can get—especially if it's with an intriguing lycan who's untamed nature just might be her salvation.

CALL OF THE LYCAN SERIES

Call of the Sea
Call of the Untamed
Call of Temptation

The Playful Prince
The Bound Prince
The Rogue Prince
The Pirate Prince

❖

Captured by a Dragon-Shifter Series
Determined Prince
Rebellious Prince
Stranded with the Cajun
Hunted by the Dragon
Mischievous Prince
Headstrong Prince

❖

Space Lords Series
His Frost Maiden
His Fire Maiden
His Metal Maiden
His Earth Maiden
His Woodland Maiden

❖

Qurilixen Lords Series
Dragon Prince
Marked Prince
More Coming Soon!

❈

To learn more about the Qurilixen World series of books and to stay up to date on the latest book list visit www.MichellePillow.com

AUTHOR UPDATES

To stay informed about when a new book in the
series installments is released, sign up for updates:

michellepillow.com/author-updates

To Rocky, who firmly believe she was helping me every time her paw hits my keyboard. To Bella Monster, my 'think tank', who swears she's not sleeping even though her eyes are never open during work sessions and all her suggestions sounds like snores. To Fiona, who is in charge of us all.

PROLOGUE

Unknown Shores
Middle Ages

ANGRY WAVES LASHED out from the depths of the ocean, as the old sea witch pointed her finger toward the shore. Ceana's body was smashed upon the rocks, her gown long since tattered from being tossed about at the water's dangerous whims. Death was close. She could feel it closing in on her. At this point she welcomed it. Kerrigan was safe. The witch had released him. She'd accomplished what she'd set out to do.

But who was going to save her?

Ceana didn't bother to lift her head as water rushed over it. It hurt to breathe, which worked to her advantage as it kept the water out of her lungs. The wave pulled back, dragging her limp body along the sandy shore. Her flesh was raw from the rough texture of the pebbles grinding against it and the wounds stung unmercifully from the salt water. The night was warm, the moon full. She had no idea where the witch had brought her, but the shore did not remind her of the rocky crags of her homeland in Scotland and the sea was definitely warmer. At the moment, she'd almost welcome the icy numbness that came from the ocean along the cliffs.

The water rushed over her again and she thought of breathing it. She knew it would burn, but then it would all be over. Surely there would be a place in heaven for her after her sacrifice. The water pulled back too soon. Ceana opened her mouth, waiting. Then it happened. The ocean filled her, burning a welcome trail that would lead to the end of her suffering. It didn't hurt as bad as she thought it would. She'd been beaten to the point that death was welcome.

The pitiless cackle of the witch echoed in her head as the world darkened. Soon. Soon. Death was near. She couldn't feel her body. Her limbs became cold and then nothing.

OUTSIDE ASTORIA, OREGON,
MODERN DAY

Musicians played fiddles, the sound flowing over the beach, filling the evening with the songs of the past. Ian grinned at his brothers as he lifted a mug. They enjoyed these gatherings along the beach. The cold wind and the sound of the ocean were unfettered by modern life. It reminded them of the past, of a time when they were born into nobility. Though no matter how the world changed and shaped itself, nature stayed the same. Night was still night, they were still young men and the Earth turned ever forward.

"My lord, come! Dance with me!" called Meghan. Just like him, she was lycan born, ruled by the full moon but not controlled by it. Her lithe body moved in time to the music as her long skirt blew in the wind. Flames licked the darkening sky, glowing on her tanned flesh and jet-black hair. The wolf was in her eyes, golden and eager. Ian knew her invitation, having sampled it more than once over the centuries. She wanted to mate, wanted his hard cock to pound her into beastly submission. Only an immortal could take his rough handling, only an immortal could recover after he was done with her.

Ian's cock stirred as she swung her hips back and forth, swaying to the primal beat. It didn't take much to incite his lust. The beast in him was fierce and always ready to unleash itself to play. His heart was another matter. It stirred for no woman. Not anymore and Ian was fine with that.

When he was younger, a woman had saved him from death, pulling him from the cold depths of the ocean. It had been a night like this, with the waves thrashing against the shore. The moon had been full, just as it was now, and his blood had been to the point of boiling in his veins. Being a lycanthrope, he was called to the sea, for the moon controlled the tides just as it controlled the stirring of his blood. His emotions hit like continual waves, exciting him to a fevered pitch. The sensation was like a drug and it was also one of the reasons he liked the sea. Another was because he was born under the astrological sign of Cancer the Crab. Sometimes, he thought he had it worse than the others. He was Cancer, ruled by the moon and called to the sea, but also lycan, born of the night.

Like a true Cancerian, Ian was a patient leader and immensely loyal, which was important since he was a prince amongst his wild people. Time and distance could never lessen friendship or loyalty. And, like Cancer the Crab, when he seized an object he wanted he'd rather lose his claw than let go, and if he lost his claw, he'd only grow another and seize it again—metaphorically, of course. Also, true to the Cancer nature, he took great pride in his history, family and traditions. He guarded those things with his life and would never give up a debate or battle until he got his point across.

Ian imagined it was these traits that made him still think of the woman who saved him, even all these years later. At the time, he'd been obsessed with finding out who she was. However, as time passed he knew she had to be long dead. No mortal could live as long as his kind. His Cancerian nature refused to let go of her memory and he convinced himself that the woman was the only one who could ever hold his heart. All it took was one look at her and he'd known, as he still knew, that she was the one he could love for all time.

But his lust? Mmm, just looking at a pretty woman could bring the more base of his natures surging forth. And why shouldn't it surge forth now? After all, the future king of the lycans needed to purge the passions in his body in order to keep a level head.

He glanced up, his skin tingling. It was almost completely dark. The sun was close to setting, just barely peeking over the horizon. Clouds passed over the full moon—a moon that called him to shift. He could resist, would resist for the time being. Already some of his fellow lycans howled, partly shifted as they drank far into their cups.

It was early yet. By midnight the beach would become an orgy of the flesh. Meghan's large breasts bounced in the combination of moonlight, fire and the setting sun. She wore a small bikini top that overflowed with her superior attributes. Ian licked his lips, feeling very beastly indeed.

"...lest Meghan better watch out."

Ian turned to his brother, James, barely catching his words. He grinned, knowing the guys were giving him a hard time for staring like the beast he was. In truth, any one of them would take Meghan to their bed but Ian knew they didn't. She refused them, choosing to save herself for him. He knew she wanted to be queen of the clans someday. Who knew, perhaps he would marry her. What else was he going to do? Pine for a woman whose face he couldn't recall?

Guilt assaulted him when he thought of her. The woman had saved his life. The least he could do was remember every detail of her pretty face. Ian closed his eyes, bringing forth her image the best he could. The exact details were a blur now, but he had the list in his mind. The moment had been brief, a flash in the middle of the night nearly a century ago. Long blonde waves almost silver by the light of the moon had surrounded him. Storm-weathered eyes, so round and large, shone in her perfect white skin. Her face was white as the snow, her lips red as blood.

Ian tried, but her face was still blurred by time. Her lips parted and she'd asked him something.

When were you born?

To this day, he didn't know what she had meant by that.

Laughter rose around him, and he opened his eyes.

James slapped him on the back, grinning. "Liquor too stout for you, brother?"

"Your jokes are too bad," Roark, the youngest of the three O'Connell brothers, said from their side. He looked like his older siblings, though was slightly shorter in stature and chose to wear his hair long to his waist, instead of short like Ian and James. Ian's own dark brown locks were chopped off at his shoulders and James' were cut even shorter than that— falling to just above his chin.

All of them had the broad shoulders and muscular bodies prevalent in their kind, especially the natural born. Humans who were changed were often slightly smaller because of their mortal heritage. The lycans took pride in themselves, in staying groomed and honoring their place in the lycan community, though they did have distinctly different styles. Ian preferred slacks and lightweight sweaters. James favored jeans and T-shirts and, much to his brothers' teasing, Roark wore leather—lots and lots of studded, black, biker-style leather.

They were an ancient people, their race as old as the human society, growing with the humans from a time when mortals knew of all the supernatural races. They used to be hunted, condemned as evil by the church. Sure, times were wilder in the early days, but so it was with all the races—mortal and supernatural. Just as humans no longer roamed the countryside pillaging and wielding swords, so did his people no longer wildly wield tooth and fang.

Now humans denied their existence, which suited most of them just fine. Occasionally, lines would be blurred and mortals would be turned. Lycans were lusty creatures after all, craving both blood and sex. Circumstances had to be right, the bloodline perfect, the moon full, for the bite to take effect. It was against the law to turn mortals. A lycan could attack fifty humans and only one would possibly start to turn, so if one was turned the odds were that lycan had attacked many before the changed one. Even then, it didn't guarantee they'd make it through the horrifically painful process. It's why his kind didn't mate with humans. Sure, they slept with them, dated them, some even spent lifetimes with them, but they didn't mate with them, not for all eternity. Only other immortal supernaturals were suitable lifemates. Too many lycans had seen their loved ones die as they tried to turn them. It was a painful memory that would be carried into eternity. For, if not murdered, the lycan would live forever.

Ian's brother helped to track down the rogue wolves who feasted on mortals, those who broke their laws—meager laws as they were. James was especially good at helping the newly turned to cope with their new gifts. He had a delicate way about him that the young ones responded to. Luckily, it had been many years since James' skill was called upon. The clan had been peaceful for the most part.

Thinking of feasting and sex, Ian looked at Meghan.

"I will gladly pursue her if she is too much lycan for you," Roark offered when Meghan pouted her lips at Ian for not coming to her as she beckoned him to do.

"Ah, you have no chance with that. She only parts her thighs for Ian. Her pussy is too refined for the likes of us," James grumbled. "You better watch yourself, brother, or you'll find yourself married to Meghan yet."

Ian raised a brow at his brother's distemper. It was no secret that James didn't like the woman. Sure, he'd fuck her if she offered—just like any of the males would—but he wouldn't like her as he was doing it.

"Relax," Ian said, laughing softly at James' suddenly foul mood.

"I'll relax when you cast her aside," James said. "That woman is too hungry for power—your power. I would not bow to her as my queen. Her heart is not pure and it definitely does not love you, just your future crown. I have no doubt that she would kill our father for the right to rule the clan."

"It's just sex, James," Ian assured him. It wasn't the first time he had done so. "Meghan knows that I do not love her as I have told her before."

"Then why bother?" Roark asked. "Take Brona or Dana. With the O'Connell charm I am sure they'd be most willing to bed you."

"Brona?" Ian shivered. "She's just now a century, merely a babe."

"And Dana's father is too protective of her," James said. "I would not have her father causing us trouble."

"Then how about Deirdre from the Macintyres? Or Padraigin MacConchobhair?" Roark offered, grinning in private thought.

"Padra?" James said. "Yes, she would make a fine choice."

Ian lifted a brow. "Play matchmaker with each other. I have an itch that I want Meghan to suck."

"I believe the word is scratch," Roark offered helpfully with a flip of his hair.

"Oh, she does that too." Ian winked, thrusting his mug over to James.

"But why her?" James protested.

Ian grinned. "Just look at her breasts."

Roark howled, James rolled his eyes and Ian made a move toward the sexy lycan in question. James didn't have to like Meghan. She was in Ian's bed, not his brother's. And the woman did enjoy sex —oral, anal, in any position he could bend her in. Why shouldn't he go to her?

When were you born?

Ian paused in mid-prowl. His head twitched to the side, listening past the fiddles and the flames, stretching out over the ocean waves. That voice. It was clearer now, not like before. It was as if he was hearing her for the first time.

Your name?

Ian tensed. He'd never caught her name, but part of him called out with his mind, hoping to give a name to the memory.

Who are you? Please. Answer me. Ask me again!

"Mmm, Your Royal Highness, why you gotta make a girl beg for it?"

Ian looked down as Meghan slid next to him. He hated when she called him "your royal highness" and such. It was only a reminder that she saw his title and his cock, not the man beneath both. But who was he to be picky when he was aroused and she was will-ing? Her nipples were already hard as they hit his chest. She rubbed her bikini-clad chest along his, until he could feel the buds though the thin material of his crimson sweater.

"Oh, Majesty, you seem to have an affliction. Come with me and let me tend to you." Flames glinted off her jet-black locks as she ran her hand down his chest to his stiff, protruding mass of flesh. Grasping his cock, her breathing deepened. Her eyes flashed completely golden. "You want to play tonight, don't you? I can feel the wolf starting to expand inside your pants. Come with me. Let me attend you, my prince. I will let you unleash the wolf tonight. I will let you take me as the beast."

Ian's nostrils flared. Meghan's feminine scent was strong and he knew her to be so wet that her bikini bottoms would be soaked with her cream. His body was willing, but his spirit was holding back. A feeling of mild disgust curled in him and he couldn't figure out why tonight, out of so many, he should find Meghan mildly repulsive.

Was it James' words? Was he tired of Meghan?

Tell me, when were you born?

No, it was her. He was sure he'd heard it that time. It couldn't be his imagination. Not again. She was human, he'd sensed it on her. But then how did she live so many years?

"Mmm," Meghan giggled, moving to wrap her

arms around his neck. Ian grabbed her arms, stopping her. His eyes darted into the darkness, straining to see over the endless blue-black waves. The sun set completely, the edge of its golden purple light giving way to the blue of moonlit darkness. His body was tense, ready to run, to shift if he had to use more of his abilities.

The sea called to him and the moonlight shot into his skin, burning him. Sounds invaded him, becoming so loud he couldn't hear past the undulation of the waves, the faint sound of sand shifting over the beach with each powerful hit of the ocean. The sound of droplets spraying over the air became clear to him, like the tingling of ice in a glass. Ian tensed, waiting to hear it again, to hear her. The woman. His woman.

This can't be a dream.

"Ian?" Meghan gasped, confusion in her tone.

Ian pushed her back, irritated that she dared to enter his head with her voice. She stumbled and he instantly felt sorry, but he was too afraid to take his concentration off the distance.

"Ian!" Meghan demanded, her tone a hiss of breath as she growled at him in warning.

"You're not the one I want," he said, absently, not paying attention to the woman. The subtle sound of laughter rang all around him, distorted like a bad hallucination. In the distance he heard James and Roark above all others. He shut them out, again waiting for the water to give him its secrets.

Do you play tricks on me, ocean? Why do you call me to your depths? She cannot be there. She cannot.

A sensation washed over him. It was a strange feeling, but one he had known before. The urge was mindlessly beckoning him into the depths of the water. It had been the same that night he had almost died. The sea called him to her and he'd gone willingly into the murky waters only to be sucked in by the current. This time he held back. He was stronger now, could resist the call.

He could resist.

Ian slowly began walking.

"You will not disregard me!" Meghan roared, leaping up. The hot-tempered lycan female lunged for him. Without thought, Ian lifted his arm and grabbed her mid-strike and threw her to the ground behind him. Meghan grunted, but he knew she wasn't hurt. It would take more than a little rough-housing to hurt her. No, if anything, Meghan's pride was the only thing bruised by him this night.

Meghan's scream turned into a loud roar of anger. He glanced behind to see her bikini on the ground and the dark, furry silhouette of her shifted form running into the darkness. Her paws kicked up sand. The woman was angry, but he could deal with her later. James was right. It was time he called off any sexual relationship with Meghan. By attacking him openly, she had overstepped her bounds. He had no desire to punish her for it, but her insubordination could not be allowed.

Ian could not be weak.

And still, he kept walking, strongly drawn to the sea.

"Ian?" James called.

Ian managed to lift his hand.

"More for us!" Roark's voice rose up, inciting boisterous cheers. Ian appreciated his brothers, knowing instinctively that they were drawing attention away from him and giving him time alone—as they assumed he so obviously wanted. No doubt James would gladly give him an eternity alone for opening rejecting Meghan.

Ian began to jog, following his gut instincts along the shore. The water hit his feet, so icy cold. It was a shock to his warmer blood, but he didn't care. He kept going.

Where are you? Where are you?

His mind called out to her. He felt her now. It

had to be her. He got the same feeling moments before the ocean pulled him. Ian slowed, changing directions in the water. His knees rose high as he marched away from shore. The water sloshed over his waist until his legs no longer surfaced with each step. His arms swayed, scooping the water as if he could get away from the sandy beach all the faster.

A wave hit him, knocking him down as the sea swallowed him into its depths. The current pulled his body, washing him into the darkness. Reality hit him and he started to struggle. But even with his lycan strength, he could not beat the will of the ocean. Each punch, every kick only shifted the water. He was drowning.

3

AFTER ENDLESS DAYS and nights adrift in the water, she knew how to navigate the current. Her body was strong and she was close to shore. Just a few more strokes and she would be there—safe on land for another long, moon-filled night. Ceana swam for shore. She had lost track of time, not realizing that the full moon was this night.

She hated full moons, hated being forced onto land to wait them out. It was her curse to find port each time the round, celestial globe showed itself fully. On those nights, she turned back to her old human form. The brief times out of the water were only a cruel reminder of how much she'd lost.

Sensing a shift in the water by her legs, she

stopped swimming and let the wave ride her up and down over the turbulent surface. Closing her eyes, she knew someone was in trouble. She'd saved enough drowning humans in her time to know what the sounds of a dying one was.

Diving down, she easily found a hand and pulled. What was a man doing in the water, alone, at this time of night? She tugged him up, cursing his heavy weight. Even though he would tire her, she couldn't let him go. Something in her, some bit of humanity she had left kept her from letting him drown.

Maybe this one will be it?

Ceana cursed the thought for entering her head. No, this one wasn't it. None of them were it. There was no ending to her moonlit curse. The sea witch had seen to that long ago, when she stood above the broken human Ceana had been, cursing her for an eternity.

He is not the one. I should save him and leave him on shore. From there he is on his own.

Ceana swam, pulling the man's unusually heavy weight behind her. He was a big man and she wished for her fins. With her tail she'd be able to drag him much easier. But no, the moon had already changed her legs into human limbs. Grunting for breath, she pulled him behind her as her human lungs burned and her muscles ached. Even when she tired, she did not give up.

"Awaken!" she ordered, speaking the language used by the mainlanders in the area. It was one of the rare gifts in her curse. She spoke whatever language of the shore she was closest to. "Help save yourself. Swim."

The order revived him some and she felt him kicking his legs in long strokes behind them. They surged forward, making better time now that he helped. The man moaned, the sound sending chills over her, like a sound from her past. But that was crazy. Everyone she'd ever loved was dead. If only she could die and join them, but no. The dangerous creatures of the sea didn't dare touch her. Not even the sharks would eat her if she bled right in front of them like a willing sacrifice. The sea witch saw to that. Even now, if she were to drown in her human form, she'd suffer greatly and find herself alive in the morning, sick for weeks but very much alive.

"Come on," she gasped, "wake up! Save yourself."

The man growled as she dug her fingernails into

his skin. He jolted out of her grasp, the force of his body's weight pulling her under. She floundered beneath the dark surface, trying to grab the flailing man beneath the water before the current swept him away.

Damn human! Stop struggling. Stop it now! I'm trying to help you.

In the breadth of a second, time stood still as they were under the waves. A stream of moonlight lit the area just enough for her to see his face clearly. The man stopped kicking as he stared at her. His dark eyes reflected the moon above, taking on a silver cast. His dark hair drifted around his head and he looked awed more than scared.

Ceana knew she was considered a great beauty to mortal men. The ones she'd passed over the years made their desire for her exceedingly clear. It took her a century, naïve fool that she was, to discover that lust and love were two entirely different things. Sure the men on shore said they loved her, were convinced of it, but after they had their way the curse remained. Some even went mad searching the ocean for her. She knew because she followed their ships, hoping they'd catch her, convincing herself if she said she loved them and pretended to mean it they would be the ones to free her from her watery prison.

Later, she came to realize that their obsession with her was just part of her mermaid allure—a magic charm of sorts. Just another ironic twist to the sea witch's evil curse. She would search an eternity for love strong enough to break the curse, but would only find those enraptured by a spell. No doubt this one would say he loved her as well as soon as she dragged him onto shore.

Ceana looked him over in the moonlight. He was handsome, with a strong face and a nice, tight body. Again she felt a tug of the familiar in him, but maybe she'd just seen too many faces over the years that all human males started to look alike. If she'd seen one, she'd seen them all, or so it seemed.

Her body tingled with the beginning stir of desire. She'd given up long ago being ashamed of her natural responses to the male gender. Her human upbringing taught her that sex was bad. But really, what was going to happen to her that was worse than what had been done?

The man's eyes started to close. A cloud passed over the moon, darkening the waters once more. Ceana jerked back into action. She grabbed the front of his shirt and pulled him up with her, breaking the surface. The man came instantly to his senses, flailing as he gasped for breath. Yellow-tinted eyes found hers and she thought the color a trick of the moonlight and water.

Ceana glanced up at the sky. There was something almost strange and golden to the moon this night. She didn't have time to contemplate. Her limbs were cold and she was starting to wear out.

"Swim," she ordered hoarsely, her throat sore from swallowing the briny water.

The man obeyed, coughing as if he would speak. Ceana pumped her arms, not giving him time to respond. Now was not the time to hear how much he wanted her, how beautiful she was. They all said that. Glancing over her shoulder several times, she made sure he was behind her.

It felt like an eternity before her feet hit shore, and Ceana knew a little bit about waiting an eternity. She breathed deeply, falling down as soon as she could do so without going under. As soon as her hands hit sand, she was grabbed around the waist and lifted up into the air.

"I got you, sweetheart, don't worry." The man was carting her toward shore. Whenever she shifted, she wasn't left with clothing and his shirt stuck to her naked stomach. His arm was around her waist, holding her against the side of his body. The water on her skin caused his hand to slip and it grazed along the underside of her breast. She breathed deeply, dazed by the heat that unfurled from his touch. Her body was stiff and icy and he felt like he was on fire.

Fever?

Ceana couldn't help herself as she burrowed into his warm, strong body. The man carried her out of the water to shore only to set her down on her feet. They both instantly collapsed in the sand, gasping for air. Breathing hard, Ceana turned and looked at him. His dark eyes stared into hers.

"You'll have to be more careful," he said. There was a soft accented burr to his words, reminding her of the voices of her past. He sounded Gaelic. "What are you doing that far out from shore without any clothing? Are you shipwrecked?"

"You sound as if you rescued me, when it is I who pulled you from the water. Believe me, the ocean cannot hurt me," Ceana whispered. Her long hair stuck to her skin.

"I did save you. I went in the water when I heard you call." The man sat up, still breathing heavy, as he pulled his wet shirt off and tossed it aside. The moonlight caressed the planes of his hard, muscular chest, gleaming off the hard nipples and rippling over the tight stomach like waves against the shore. "I went into the water to rescue you."

Ceana followed suit, sitting on the grainy sand. She brushed off her skin and laughed. "I did not call out for rescue, I assure you. Let me guess. You were drinking on the shore with your friends and decided to take a swim. You're not the first one I've come across who's been so foolish. Next time, stay on shore."

When he didn't answer, she looked at him. His eyes were filled with gold and he was staring at her chest. She glanced down, reminded of her nudity. Looking up, she saw him lick his lips. It was a slow, deliberate gesture. His muscles tensed, as if ready to pounce.

He didn't look at her eyes, but let his gaze instead travel over her body. His eyes stopped when they reached the soft golden curls hiding her pussy from view. Again he licked his lips, his nostrils flaring ever so slightly. The dark color of his eyes changed completely, glowing like liquid gold.

"You are...?" she paused, trying to remember the word she was looking for. Back when she was a girl, there had been a man in her village that was like him. She'd been scared of him, but then she hadn't been immortal at the time. "What is the word?"

"Aroused?" he offered, his hot gaze darting up to hers. The man was completely unashamed by the fact. "Yes, very. And by the sweet smell of your desire I detect building between your thighs so are you."

Ceana didn't deny it for it was true. She was turned on by him. With only one night of full moon she never had time to be picky or wait to get to know a man. And this one was certainly intriguing. What harm was there in finding mutual release?

"Mmm, yes, but I meant you are...a beast. Right? Part man, part four legs. Ah," she paused, wrinkling her nose, trying to remember the right word. So much she remembered, adapting easily with the times, but other things were harder. Rarely did she discuss animals with humans. "Mongrel."

The man flinched. "Wolf."

"Yes, you are a wolf-man, are you not?"

"You know about lycans?" He seemed surprised. "But you are human."

Ceana nodded. "We had one in our village when I was little."

"And yet you are not afraid of me?"

Knowing that time was short and not wanting to tell him too much, lest he discover she was not really from his time, she slowly crawled forward, going closer to him. "I assure you, wolf man, there is nothing you can do to me that will harm me."

His expression became almost primal as his eyes again darted down to her breasts. The moonlight caressed his tanned flesh and wet clothing.

"Give me your name, wolf, so I know what to scream when you are taking me." Ceana wanted to laugh at his shocked look, but held back.

"I-Ian," he stuttered.

"Mmm, Ian. Perfect. I am Ceana." Without waiting, she lunged forward and pressed her mouth to his. She shoved her tongue into his mouth and the sweet taste of him made her moan. The man fell onto his back in the sand, gripping her hips. Ceana straddled him with her thighs, jolting with pleasure at the way his tight stomach rubbed along her pussy. The texture of the sand scratched as he kneaded his fingers over her flesh, but the grainy annoyance wasn't enough to cause her pain. Besides, she was too lost in his touch to care.

Ceana rubbed her breasts along his chest. He was so warm that her body practically drank in his heat. Knowing he was part wolf turned her on. How could she pass up an experience like this? Especially when Ian moved his lips so expertly and when his touch was so damned powerful?

Animalistic sounds came from him and he grabbed her forcibly by the hips, pulling her pussy down against his clothed cock. The thick shaft pressed tightly against his wet pants and he ground her against it, rocking her as he arched back. The gesture broke their kiss. Ian growled loud and long, pulling and pushing her wildly as if he couldn't stop. His cock only grew bigger with each pass.

Ceana clawed his chest, liking the wild ride too much to protest. She just let him have his way, unable to really do anything to stop his superior strength. His beautiful body worked beneath hers, the muscles rippling like a beautiful current under her hands. His face hardened and fangs sprouted between his lips. With a roar, he trembled. The length of his hair grew, fanning out over his face. His eyes yellowed and glowed with an exciting power and danger. Little hairs spouted out of his chest and she curled her fingers into them, holding on as he worked her toward a tumultuous climax.

"Ah," she cried, shaking violently against the hard mass pressing into her. The friction stimulated her clit until she could take no more. Ian jerked as she came and she wondered if he was releasing himself into his pants.

"Ceana," he growled in the back of his throat, only to whisper. "It's you, isn't it? You're who I've been looking for."

"I sure am," she said in response to his odd love-talk. "I'm exactly who you've been looking for."

4

IAN COULDN'T BELIEVE his luck as he stared in awe at the woman above him. She was human, he smelled that clearly, but it was her. She had to be the one! Ceana was the woman he'd been searching for. He'd suspected that moment in the water, when they were both under and she'd stared at him. Her eyes had taken on the silver light of the moon.

But, he wasn't sure until he saw her face, as she rode above him in passion, her hair drying in golden long waves about her pale, perfect skin. It was her. She was alive and had taken him again from the depths of the ocean.

Reincarnated?

Time travel?

Did it matter?

His cock throbbed beneath her, ready for more. How did this happen? Was he dead? Dreaming? Insane? Again, what did it matter? The human woman was on top of him, her gorgeous body naked and proud and willing to do his bidding. The beast desperately wanted to come out and play, but he kept it back. He would not hurt her, couldn't hurt her.

"You are not..." She hesitated, looking down in what could only have been disappointment. "You are not done, are you? That is it?"

The woman had just come, screaming into the night and she wanted more? Ian grinned. He could definitely do more. In fact, he'd bet even money he could outlast the poor thing.

"Trust me, I can go for nights," he assured her. "You'd just better hope you don't get too tired before I'm ready to stop."

Her brow rose at the challenge and he could instantly smell how the idea excited her. Licking her lips, she stood. "Hmm, it's been a long time since I've had a man who claimed that. He was a sore disappointment."

Ian's gut tightened and a feeling of possessiveness came over him. He did not want to hear about other men being inside her body. Rolling up from the ground, he stood, his hands instantly on his pants to take them off. "By the time I'm done, you will not remember there being any others."

The woman had the nerve to laugh at his claim.

"You think that funny?" Ian pushed his pants from his hips, freeing his cock and her laughter instantly died. He grinned wickedly and grabbed his thick shaft. Her rounded eyes stared at the massive weapon he sported between his thighs. It wasn't the first time he'd gotten that reaction. An enormous cock and the innate ability to know how to wield it was just another perk of being Prince of the Lycans.

"*Ahhh*," she breathed heavily, her mouth hanging open. He stared at her full lips. They were so lush and inviting. Territorial feelings burst forth in him and he wanted to lay his scent on the woman so no other lycan would dare to touch her without his express permission.

"You dare to laugh at my claim?" The dominant beast inside him surged forth, showing itself once more in little physical signs—the hair on his chest, the longer locks about his head, the fangs, his eyes, the lengthening of his already engorged cock. Unable to control himself, he ordered her, "Crawl forward to me. Show me how much you want me. Take my cock in your mouth and suck it so I come in your throat."

If it had been any woman from his clan, she'd

have done so instantly, excitedly, willingly. This woman arched a brow at the order. "Ah, I was going to until you said that. Now you can suck your own cock."

"Ceana..."

"What?" She lay on her back and looked up at the stars. "You actually think you can order me about like that and I won't take offense? Crawl to me? Like I am some cuttlefish following the school? I don't care who or what you are, Ian, I refuse to have my life controlled." Then under her breath, she said, "My life is too controlled as it is without you telling me what to do."

"I am a prince among my people," he said, unsure what to say to the rest. No one had ever questioned his command before.

"And I'm queen of the ocean," she returned. "So I think you should bow to me."

"I do not bow to women," he exclaimed. Ian glanced around, tempted to do just that if it meant getting her back into his arms. What a fool he was! But he couldn't help it. It was in his nature to dominate. He didn't sense any of his clan around and turned back to her.

"Then, you might want to continue up the beach." Ceana put her hands behind her head and bent her knees, bathing in the moonlight. Her thighs parted, giving him a full view of her wet pussy. "I'm sure there is some weak-minded lady just waiting for a stud like you to make her night."

Ian didn't move. She was serious!

"Go on, then," she said. "Shoo."

Ian growled. The woman jolted some but didn't change her position on the ground. "You think you can dismiss me that easily?"

Pushing up on her elbows, she whispered, "Crawl to me. Show me how serious you are." She parted her thighs wider.

Ian cursed himself, even as he fell to his knees and crawled forward. Lust ran rampant through him, fueled by the moon and the sea. Damn his Cancerian nature! How easily his body was influenced by both. And the sexy goddess, who'd emerged from the ocean like a gift from his rulers, didn't do much for his control.

Ian crawled to her, nipping at her thigh as he was drawn to lick her pussy. Letting his long tongue flick, he got his first taste of her sweetness. He meant to tease her into submission, but that one taste left him mindless for more. Licking, he did it again and again, each time pressing harder until his mouth was flat against her clit and he was sucking and working her body for all it had.

Ceana grabbed his hair, pulling it hard as she bucked against him. He pushed her legs open wider with a confident shove, licking and sucking at her wet clit, nibbling it. His tongue worked along her folds, probing and pushing just right. Only when she was crying out for more, begging him to let her come, did he give her what she needed. Her cries rang out over his head. Ian slipped his tongue into her, getting an intimate taste. Her body clutched him, as she shook with a rocky climax.

❖

CEANA BREATHED HARD, amazed at the force with which he commanded her body. She knew he wouldn't leave, not in the middle of what they were about. No man would. They were simple creatures in that way—even this sexy wolf man.

Ian pulled away from her, instantly moving up her body. She let him explore, enjoying the rough feel of his mouth on her chest. He devoured her breasts, nicking her with his teeth. It stung, but felt so good she wanted him to do it again. Amazedly, when he was between her thighs, he'd only given her pleasure, not pain. Ian groaned, licking the wound before sucking a good portion of her breast deep into his hot mouth.

"I want you to suck me," he said against her chest. "Please."

"That's better," she purred, pushing him over. Little grains of sand fell down her back as she rose above him. "That's a good little wolf man."

Ceana crawled down his body. His arousal strained, thick with need, over the soft globes of his balls. She stroked it several times with her hands, feeling the impossibly huge length of it. Then, leaning over, brought the ruddy tip of his shaft to her mouth. She licked the cock head, swirling her tongue.

It was a strange game they played. But she loved that she had complete command over him. There was freedom in being with Ian, but also a sadness because it wouldn't last past one night. She could do anything because tomorrow it wouldn't matter. There were no commitments, no unnecessary talk of love and emotions. It was like they had a silent understanding. They both needed to be touched, to feel, to fuck. This was just pure, animalistic sex. It was all it could ever be.

She took his balls in her hand. Squeezing gently,

she elicited a moan of masculine approval. Slowly, she trailed her lips down one side of his shaft with light, tormenting kisses only to come back up the other.

"Ah, sweet torment," he growled, gripping at the sand on either side of him. His fist hit the ground hard several times and his body tensed.

Finally, she took him into her mouth. Her teeth lightly grazed along his shaft as she fitted him as deep as he would go. She kept one hand on his balls, the other on his shaft to help accommodate his giant length.

He grunted in satisfaction as she blew lightly and sucked heavily in turn. Ceana sucked harder and he growled. His hands dove into her hair and jerked her down hard, nearly gagging her with his length. She pulled back and he did it again before she could brace her hands to the ground. With a yell, he came, squirting seed down her throat as he held her mouth to his cock. The salty taste of him was too good and she didn't protest as she swallowed him down.

Ceana had to admit his need to control excited her. It was a battle of the wills, one she knew neither of them would win. Too bad there wasn't more time to play. Already the moon was traveling across the sky. Soon she would be driven back into the ocean to live out her fate.

He let go and she pulled off with a gasp. Ian looked concerned, even through his passion-hazed features. "Did I hurt you?"

"I told you," she said, crawling on top of him and resting against his naked, warm body. She lay still as their bodies cooled and their heartbeats returned to normal. It was nice to be held. She really missed the closeness of human contact, the companionship, just hearing another voice. Taking a deep breath, she finished softly, "There is nothing you can do that will cause me harm."

❧

CEANA SIGHED, resting on Ian in the aftermath of their pleasure. His cock lay sated along his thigh, only slightly engorged as it pressed against her. His muscled chest rippled gorgeously beneath his tanned flesh and she cuddled into him. A cool breeze came from the ocean, but he was warm enough for the both of them. She liked the feel of his muscles beneath her cheek. In fact, she felt so relaxed she fell asleep. When she awoke, it was to the gentle kneading of

Ian's hands on her lower back and the poke of his rising shaft against her lower stomach.

His mouth nuzzled her neck, as he lightly kissed her. His voice deep and a little hoarse, "Did you get enough rest?"

Ceana mumbled, managing to get out, "Mmm-hmm."

"Are you ready for more?" She looked up at him. He was still breathing hard but he managed to give her a lopsided grin.

"Mmm-hmm," Ceana answered with a laugh, snuggling against him once more.

"Good, my ocean queen, because I want to give you more. Much more."

Ceana stiffened. His tone was different. It wasn't quite as domineering and it had become almost tender, caressing. No, she was just sleepy and sated. That was all. Nothing had changed. This was still just a fling. The words implied nothing.

Unless he, like the others, thinks to be falling in love with me.

Regret washed over her and he stiffened, as if sensing it.

"What? What's wrong?"

"Do not love me," she said.

"What?" he sounded surprised.

"I don't want you falling in love with me." She looked up, showing him with her expression just how serious she was. "Nothing will come of this. Nothing ever comes of this."

"Mmm, why don't we talk about it in the morning," he said, his tone low with meaning. Ceana couldn't help but laugh as he pushed his cock along her thigh. "I want to give you something first. Then you can tell me all about how I can't fall in love with you and why a relationship would never work out between us and how we're just too different—you human, me lycan."

"Ian—"

"Later," he hushed.

"Fine, later." Ceana knew there would be no later. If he refused to hear her now, what could she do about it? He'd discover there was no later soon enough—like when he awoke in the morning, completely abandoned. Hopefully, he'd convince himself she was just a dream.

"You're not regretting this, are you?" he asked.

"Mmm, no," she answered. It was partly true. She didn't regret it in the way he meant. She did regret that it could only be one night, that in the morning her curse would renew itself and she'd find herself alone in the dark, cold ocean. Ceana glanced up at him and smiled, not pulling away from his strong chest. "There are so few pleasures in life. I don't see a reason to regret what ones we do get."

"That's a very bleak outlook."

"Shhh," she ordered, covering his mouth with her hand. To emphasize her meaning, she reached between his thighs and grabbed his cock. She ran her fingers over the length the best she could in her position. It pulsed with life in her palm. "I don't want to talk about this anymore. There is so little night left. I want to play."

Ian opened his mouth and sucked a couple fingers between his teeth. Pleasure shot into her, moving like liquid ecstasy down her arm to her breasts then farther to her sex. Tingling erupted between her thighs as they eagerly came to attention.

"I like the sweet smell of your pussy, Ceana," he said, the words muffled by her hand. "And I liked the taste even more."

She began the thorough process of kissing the span of his chest. Stopping by each nipple, she licked the little buds hard. Straddling his naked waist, she rubbed her swollen clit along his hard stomach and skated her fingers over his neck and chest, tickling him with the light caress. He visibly shivered and his eyes narrowed in golden response.

"I like your eyes," she whispered. Never had she felt so free, so open with someone. "They're so dangerous and powerful. I bet nothing could hurt you."

"There are things." His tone was absent as his eyes closed.

"The ocean," she said, remembering how she saved him. His muscles strained beautifully and the heat radiating off his chest warmed her hands as they brushed against him.

"Yes, that is one of the few."

Lifting her arms over her head, she stretched, lengthening her body as she rocked her hips back and forth on his stomach. He stared at her breasts, watching them bounce with her gentle movements.

"This is torture," he growled, reaching for her breasts. His hot gaze stared into her.

Ceana laughed, bringing her arms down to touch him once more. Her ass slid back, hitting his erection. It pressed into her and she wiggled against it. His cock was indeed fiery hot. Her sex stung at the intimate contact. She gasped as he grabbed her face and pulled her roughly to his mouth. Her heart lurched. Tremors hit her, shivering a wayward path over her skin. She'd never been so aroused in her life. Ian kissed her deep, stealing her already ragged breath.

He moved her easily as they made love, touching her everywhere, roaming his hands over her flesh as he worked his mouth from one breast to the other. He stared up at her, a ravenous smile on his handsome features. His eyes glistened with the threat of his lycan side. Pleasure racked through her body as he gently sucked her nipples. She was awash with sensations, the salty smell of the sea, the pleasure of his touch. Moisture ran in a hot torrent down her thighs.

Ian flipped her over so his weight was pressing her into the sand. He rubbed his cock along her hip, searing her with his heat. She parted her thighs, eager for that first thrust. The whole night had built to this moment, this time when he would show her just how much her body could take of the powerful wolf man. Her stomach tensed, as she became almost frightened by the size of him. His cock had choked her mouth and she knew it would fill her pussy to the brink.

With a groan, Ian stretched her, easing his cock head into her. Suddenly, he stopped moving, stiffening. His muscles became as hard as rocks. More of the dark brown fur covered his skin and long teeth grew from his mouth until he was almost every inch a lycan. The scene should have scared her, but Ceana found it did quite the opposite. It aroused her further. The tip of his cock stretched her wider and she knew that part of him grew as well. He was breathing hard, panting as if he was seconds away from pounding roughly into her. His golden eyes focused on her, full of questions.

"Do it." Ceana didn't know what prompted the whisper to escape her lips. Maybe it was the knowledge that this may never happen again. Maybe it was the night air, or the full moon. "Don't be afraid. Fuck me."

His muscles flexed as he angled his hips to hers. Slowly, Ian thrust his hard cock inside her, prying her apart with his heavy length. Ceana gasped as he filled her up. She rocked her hips, working him in shallow strokes as he broke her open to him. Thrusting up, she took him to the hilt. Ian roared and lost control. In a frenzy, he took her, pumping his hips fast and hard into her. Ceana moaned, calling for more.

The fit, combined with their night full of love play was too much. Ceana shook, orgasming so hard her teeth chattered. Ian howled, stiffening inside her as he released his seed. A long moment passed before Ian moved and regained control over his body. His breathing slowed down and his body gradually made the transformation back from the wolf man. When he looked completely human once more, except for his dangerously lit eyes, he pulled out of her and collapsed at her side.

A soft moan left her lips and she mumbled incoherently, not even sure what it was she was trying to say to him. All she knew is that she felt good—really good. Ian cradled her in his arms.

"I can't stay too much longer," she whispered, closing her eyes. "Morning approaches."

"Just try to get away," he answered, holding her tighter.

5

CEANA AWOKE WITH A JOLT. Breathing hard, she looked from Ian's slumbering, naked body to the sunrise. The rays were just beginning to peek over the horizon. Panicked, she turned back to look at Ian once more. He was gorgeous, the soft orange glow of morning caressing his tanned flesh. A small, almost lecherous smile curled the sides of his lips, but his eyes were closed.

Her heart beat heavily in her chest. She didn't want to leave him, but with the sunrise she had no choice. It wouldn't do to be discovered as a mermaid on land. She'd be unable to defend herself and the surface air would dry out her fins, causing great pain.

Besides, what would Ian do if he discovered what she was?

She licked her lips, wanting to kiss him. But, did she dare wake him to say goodbye? At the thought, her heart twinged and she felt tears stinging her eyes. Ceana didn't want to say goodbye. She was tired of the ocean, of swimming, of leaving. She wanted to stay on land.

Touching a lock of his sand-caked hair, she mouthed, "Until another life, sweet man wolf."

What more was there to say?

Ceana stood, having no intention of waking him. Let him think her a dream, or a one-night stand. She didn't want him looking for her in the sea, didn't want him to know what she was—a cursed mermaid. Her stomach knotted as the sadness overwhelmed her, and as she walked the pain seared her deep inside. It didn't matter. She could well live with the ache for the memory of creating it would last forever.

The wind blew her dry hair, knocking the granules of sand off her body. The salty smell of the ocean was all around, punctuated by the call of birds. In the distance, rocks jutted out of the water. She hadn't seen them in the night, but now their outlines grew clearly up from the watery surface. Seashells, sand dollars and long strings of seaweed lined the shoreline, having been washed up in the night. There was even a shark's tooth, its black outline stark against the bleached sand. Stepping into a tidal pool, she purposefully missed a starfish. Leaning over, she picked it up and tossed it back out into the water where it would be safe from beachcombers. She did the same with a few live sand dollars.

Turning around, she saw Ian was still asleep, his godlike body sprawled out on the sand. The cold ocean hit her feet. She couldn't put it off much longer. It was time to go home, to her sunken ship beneath the waves where she could pretend to sit in her captain's chair and stare at the little items she'd collected over the years.

Her body straight, Ceana walked into the ocean. The waves cleaned her even as they wetted her hair. Her flesh tingled and she dove under the waves, curling her arms as she swam away from shore. She waited for her skin to change, for the fins to take over her body once more. Not thinking, she just kept going as she always did after the full moon. The water couldn't hurt her. Nothing could hurt her.

Suddenly, a cramp seized her leg. She gulped, stopping in the middle of the deep water to grab her side. Kicking, she tried to stay on the surface. But the more she kicked, the more her body tired. Ceana drifted down beneath the water, staring at her legs in shock. There was still two. Where were her fins? Her tail? Her gills? What was happening to her? She spread her arms wide, fighting back up to take breath. She'd swum far away from shore. The sun was peeking over the horizon, almost a full globe.

"Help." The sound was a whisper as she pumped her arms and legs. She started to cry. "Help!"

She was going to drown and something told her that this time there would be no coming back. Instinct kicked in and she struggled for shore. Her body ached, but she pushed on. It was no use. It was too far to swim. She was going to drown.

Gulping a lungful of air, she let out a hysterical laugh and yelled, "Finally, you old sea hag! Finally I am free of your curse!" Tears streamed over her face as she swam a little farther only to stop and float on her back. The waves rocked her back and forth. "The gods have blessed me. Do you hear me, Urbana? You can no longer have me. I am free of you, old hag. I am free of this ocean. The gods have taken pity on me and are going to let me end my life!"

Ceana laughed again. The sun shone upon her naked body as she floated on the endless sea that had been her prison for so long.

"I am no longer your prisoner," she whispered. "My death will free me."

6

THE GODS HAVE BLESSED ME. Do you hear...?

Ian frowned, sitting up. His body tingled, on guard.

...can no longer have me. I am free...

Seagulls squawked when he moved, singing their horrible sound so loud he cursed them for interrupting.

"Ceana?" His senses were alert and he stood to hear the words, so soft and faint.

The gods have taken pity on me and are going to let me end my life!

"Ceana, no! Where are you?" He looked all around the shoreline. And then, a sick feeling in his stomach, he looked at the water. Is that what she'd been doing out in the water the night before, only to stop when she saw him drowning? Was she killing herself? Is that why she slept with him so eagerly the night before? Why she claimed they could not be together in the morning, that he wasn't to love her, that she didn't want to talk about it?

His heart thundered loud in his ears. He took a deep breath, trying to pick up her scent as he charged the waters. The faintest trace of her invaded him, reminding his body of their night together. Passion stirred with fear and he mindlessly went after her to save her.

"Ceana, hold on," he said, diving beneath the surface.

I just found you again. I can't lose you now. Hold on, baby. I'm coming for you!

Churning his arms through the water, he didn't stop to think as he swam out into water. The sun was rising over the surface and he saw a glint of blonde on the water. Ceana wasn't moving, but she was floating. Then, to his horror, he watched as she slipped beneath the surface.

Acting on pure instinct and no thought for himself, he dove for her. Going deeper and deeper into the darker depths of the water, his eyes shifted to see. The salt water stung them even in their enhanced form.

He caught a glimpse of her blonde hair and reached for it. The small hold was enough. Pulling her hair, he drew her closer, grabbing another fistful of the silky locks and then another as he reeled her toward him. Ian kicked, his lungs burning, as he pulled her toward the surface. As soon as he broke the surface of the water, he hooked her about the neck and drew her up against his chest. Her already pale face was tinged with blue and her lips weren't moving. Trying to carry her and swim at the same time, he worked his way back to shore.

It seemed like forever until he got her on her back in the sand. She was still naked and the blue had worked its way down her slender frame. Running his hand over her neck, he reached to feel for her heartbeat even as he blew air into her mouth.

Ceana coughed, spouting water out of her mouth. Her eyelids fluttered only to close. She was unconscious, but Ian could hear the faint beating of her heart. Her chest rose and fell in shallow breaths.

Closing his eyes, he concentrated on his brothers, and called to them, *Roark, James!*

Ugh, yeah, I'm up! James' voice answered. Even though it was in his head, Ian knew his brother had been sleeping.

Argh, what is it? I'm busy, Roark complained.

And both of them are gorgeous.

I need you, Ian interrupted. *Now.*

Are you hurt? James demanded.

No, just come quickly. And bring a change of clothes. Ian touched Ceana's face, willing her to look at him. She didn't. But, at least she was breathing. That was something.

If you've gotten yourself into that kind of trouble, just walk it off, Roark protested. *These two are...oh, damn that feels good. Ahem, these two are really into me. I think I'm in love.*

You're always in love, said James.

And I think that your future queen may be dying! Ian screamed at them.

He felt the mindlink between them stir and knew his brothers were finally compelled into action.

You didn't, James growled. *Not Meghan! Ian, you can't. She's a conniving, manipulative—*

Damn it, just get here! Ian cut them out of his mind, not wanting to talk about it. He hadn't meant to say that Ceana would be his queen, but as he looked at her, he knew that's what he wanted. She was the woman he'd been looking for.

You have to be her, he thought. *I know you are. I finally found you again and this time I'm not letting you out of my sight.*

7

CEANA GASPED, her lungs burning from breathing in sea water. Her body was sore and battered. All around her was darkness and then she heard it. The faint cackling of Urbana behind her jolted her and she opened her eyes to see the wet sand under her hands.

"What?" She tried to push up, the scene around her all too familiar. How could this be? Was it a dream? A nightmare? Was this hell?

In horror, she turned to see the long, slender form of the witch. Her clothes washed like waves over her body and her flesh was as translucent as water. Inside her chest small eels swam where her heart should have been. Had she been human, her pale, blue face would have been beautiful. But the witch wasn't human. She was evil.

Angry waves lashed out from the depths of the ocean, as the old sea witch pointed her finger toward the shore. Ceana screamed as her body hit the rocks. Her gown was torn and as soon as she saw the crimson edging along the earthen ground, she knew where she was.

She was in the past.

Her past.

Her body ached as it had that night she was cursed. The witch came closer. She could feel the evil being. Death was close. She thought of Ian, of drowning along the shore. What now? Was she to start over? Why now? Why start over? Had she missed something along the way? Something important?

"You will pay for taking him from me!" the witch cried, as the water tossed her again.

Him?

"Kerrigan," she whispered. Her brother. He was safe. Too sore to cry, she lay with her face in the sand. It hurt to breathe, which worked to her advantage as it kept the water out of her lungs. The wave pulled back, dragging her limp body along the sandy shore. Her flesh was raw from the rough texture of the pebbles grinding against it and the wounds stung unmercifully from the salt water. The harsh cackle of the witch echoed in her head as the world darkened.

"Awaken!" the witch ordered as she flipped Ceana on her back.

A snakelike pull wrapped her ankles as the water took on a life of its own, holding her legs together. Two more magical strands of water grabbed her wrists. Even though she knew what was going to happen, she still felt the fear she'd felt the first time. The water held her, its hold like liquid shackles against her limbs that grew out in long, thick ropes to the sea. She struggled, but could not free herself. A horrible fish with sharp teeth swam up the thick tube of water that led to her body.

"Cancer, I call to you!" the witch yelled. Her body glowed, the eerie silvery blue light shining from her, into the surrounding ocean, only to craw up the liquid chains. "Help me to curse this creature who trespasses against your loyal follower."

Ceana's body was jerked higher into the air and she dangled from her shackles as if held on an invisible cross.

"By the formidable power of the Cancerian Crab, I condemn you, mortal, to immortality. You will live beneath the waves, in your brother's place. If

I can't have him, I will have you. The sea will be your home and the full moon your only respite. Only one can break this curse. One so rare you should never find him. You must find the love from one of land, born under the sign of Cancer, born of the night, ruled by the moon. Only he can break this spell. Only his pure love can set you free."

The hag cackled again, throwing her hand into the air. Droplets flew out of her as an eel jumped from her chest. Ceana screamed, but it was no use. The eel hit her face and dissipated into her body. Seconds later, purple fins sprouted from her forearms, the color threaded with soft white and silver like a seashell. The flesh of her arms was molded around it, holding the fins on. Her neck ripped open, as gills formed in her throat. She tried to claw at them, but couldn't reach them. Next, her thighs stuck together underneath her gown. Scales grew over her legs, molding them into a silvery purple tail. Finally, her feet shifted and a long caudal fin unraveled at the bottom, as thin as wet silk.

"It is done. You are mine!" Urbana yelled triumphantly. Her body burst into a million beads of water. Ceana screamed as she was flung through the air into the ocean. The water shackles let go and she sailed through the air. And, as her body hit the surface with a hard smack, she gulped.

❧

CEANA SAT UP, confused as she looked around. She was in a bed. A thick, white comforter covered her legs and a strange style of furniture was in the room. It looked like wood, but she'd never seen bedposts carved in such a way.

"Not real," she gasped, remembering her dream of the ocean. It felt real, but it couldn't be. She was safe. She was here in the...

Ceana looked around. Where exactly was she? Sun shone through large pieces of material over the windows. Spreading her legs, she found they were human. She touched her arms, running her fingers over them. Her fins were gone. Next she looked for gills. Nope. They were gone as well.

Her body was still and yet she felt dizzy. The room spun around her. Centuries had passed since she'd been in sunlight as a human—long, long centuries.

The knowledge was too much. Her body was weak from her ordeal. She let the darkness have her as she fell back on the bed.

8

Ian closed his eyes as the hot water hit his body. The warm water wasn't helping cool his ardor, but he couldn't force himself to turn the temperature down. After a night on the beach, he'd discovered sand in some unusual places. Thinking of it, he smiled, remembering the feel of his mystery woman on his cock.

His brothers were down in the kitchen, waiting for him to get cleaned up. Ian chuckled, let them wait for him. Right now, the soap felt too good against his body. Closing his eyes, he imagined that the soft lather was Ceana's hands running over him, teasing him.

Oh, how he wanted to fuck her again! Taking her hard and long, making her come over and over again.

The lycan in him begged for release. One taste of her wasn't enough. It would never be enough. He wanted more.

His cock strained, caressed by the hot water. Running his soapy hands down, he grabbed it hard, wishing it was her fingers fisting the turgid length. Turning, he hit his head hard against the shower's wall. He was too far gone in his passion to care.

Ian thrust his hips, keeping both fists closed around his cock as he pumped back and forth. The soap made them slick, just like Ceana's sweet pussy. He let the fantasy take over, squeezing and turning his hands.

In his mind, she moaned, begged, pleaded with him to take her. Ian grinned. It was a fantasy, after all.

Take me, master, the imagined Ceana begged. *Fuck me with your giant cock. Break me open. Conquer me. I am your willing slave.*

Ian groaned. He had a feeling the real Ceana would never be so submissive, but he didn't care. What he did care was that she wasn't really there. He wanted her before him.

Moaning, he jerked, spilling his seed. He fell to his knees, the hot water hitting his head. Never had masturbating done that to him—made him so weak he couldn't stand. Ian remained on the shower floor, awed by the feelings that coursed inside him for the mysterious woman.

"Ceana," he whispered, unable to do anything else. "Sweet, Ceana."

9

"ARE YOU CRAZY?" James demanded, looking across the table at Ian. "You plan on taking that woman as your bride? Did you not hear what she was mumbling all the way back from the beach?"

Ian didn't answer, as he thought of the woman upstairs in his bed. Both brothers were at his table, looking worn from a night of drinking and sex, not to mention the fact that they had to run the beach to find him and then help him cart Ceana back to town in his SUV. They also managed to get her into his bed.

She was still breathing and her color was better, but Ian was still worried. He tried to listen for her, but heard nothing. Ceana was sleeping.

Sleeping in his home, his bed.

Naked.

Ian shivered, feeling his desire for her surge forth anew. His blood was hot, near the point of boiling out of his veins. He wanted to go to her, but what could he do? She was sleeping.

Taking a deep breath, he ignored James' continuing lecture and looked around his kitchen. Ian's home was styled in the old Victorian period, popular in the Oregon coastal city. The large kitchen had high ceilings and pale cream walls that showcased one of his prized possessions—a range stove from the mid-1800s combining a broiler and an oven. True to period, the cast-iron frame was faced with gray soapstone and inlaid with brass. It required a chimney for exhaust. Bricks encased the stove in an sunken part of the wall along the side of the room. The unit wasn't really efficient to the modern era, but Ian kept it anyway. A lot of his cooking was done on flat burners hidden within the butcher block on the counter, or out on the grill. Living on the coast made seafood barbeques a way of life for him and his clan.

Parquet wood floors and large rugs covered the house. Semicircle windows arched above longer windows. Large portraits and fancy brown satin drapes graced the parlor. His brothers often teased him about his taste in décor, calling him as talented as a woman when it came to housekeeping. Ian couldn't help it if he had taste—unlike James who lived in a loft with his paintings, or Roark who preferred moving around. Every house he'd been to that Roark owned had boxes stacked in it, ready to be unpacked.

"Ian!" James demanded, drawing Ian's attention back at the hard, loud tone. "Are you even listening?"

Ian chuckled to himself. "Uh, no, not really."

Roark chuckled, taking a swig of his beer. It was early in the day, but none of them cared.

"Please, try and pay attention," James said. "The woman is crazy. You heard her. She kept talking about fish—"

"Mermaids," Roark broke in, grinning.

James sighed, continuing, "Mermaids and witches and wanting to die in the sea. Now my guess is she's escaped from an asylum and is suicidal."

"Ah, they don't call them asylums anymore," Roark offered, smiling angelically even though they all knew he was just trying to annoy James. It worked.

"I don't care what they call them. Political correctness is a bunch of crap. It's ruining our language and—"

"Here he goes again," Ian muttered to Roark. "And he calls her the crazy one."

"Fine, you asked for it. I'll be blunt." Placing his palms flat on the table, James said carefully, "If you take her as your bride and she's crazy, the O'Connell clan will not follow you. They will ridicule you as a weak future king. As much as I loathe her, Meghan would make a better choice."

Ian frowned. James often spoke with a level head when it came to matters of the clan. Sometimes he thought that James should've been in line to be king, not he. But his father once told him that James was too serious and didn't have enough heart.

Regardless, James was smart and he knew what to say to make Ian listen. The opinion of his people would persuade him. Not because he felt the need to be liked personally, but because unrest in the clan would lead to trouble and disharmony. It was hard enough keeping men ruled by the wolf in line without giving them an excuse to fight.

"James, enough, put us out of our misery already. It's too early for sermons. I only said that to aggravate you," Ian lied. "And to wake your asses up to help me."

"Are you sure? Your mark on her was strong," James insisted.

"I was drunk." Ian stood and crossed to the fridge. Roark whistled holding up his can. Grabbing a beer, Ian tossed it behind him in his youngest brother's direction. Roark caught it and popped the top in one fluid motion. "And horny."

"So you just fucked her?" James asked.

Ian closed his eyes, not letting his brothers see his expression as he hid his face behind the refrigerator door. "Fucked her" seemed so crass, but that is what he'd done, wasn't it? He'd taken her in shifted form and he'd taken her hard. As he thought of fucking her, a hard surge of desire came over him again. He'd already masturbated once in the shower to the thought of her. Taking a bottle of juice, he shut the door and pushed back his damp hair, feeling a little bit of the sand from the beach in the locks. He must have missed it when he'd been busy pleasuring himself in the shower.

"Well?" James said.

"Yeah," Ian growled. "I told you as much, now quit looking for details like a gossiping woman. When the time comes to marry, I'll make sure she's a sweet little rosebud with no problems and the makings of a queen."

"Oh, that should take you only forever," Roark mumbled.

"Roark, this one believes in mermaids," James said. "Mermaids! They just can't exist. With as long as we've been here, you know we would've seen one by now."

"I thought I saw Bigfoot once," Roark offered James. "Turned out just to be your hairy ass running in the forest."

Ian gave Roark a high five. James frowned.

"This is serious," James insisted.

"Everything with you is," Roark said. Ian kept his mouth shut. Roark was only saying what he, himself, was thinking. "You don't believe in mermaids because you've never seen them. The humans don't believe in us because they've never seen us. Are you saying that we aren't real?"

"For the love of dick! Did you just have a logical thought?" James exclaimed.

Ian laughed. "For the love of dick?"

"Is there something you'd like to tell us?" Roark asked.

James grinned. "You like that? I read it in a book where the author coined the phrase. I think it's going to catch on."

"With women, maybe," Ian said. "I don't know if you should be repeating it in front of the guys."

"What books are you reading?" Roark chuckled,

raising his brows and giving his brother a strange look.

"*Pisces Phenomenon* by Mandy M. Roth—wait, did you hear that?" James stood, his head tilted to the side.

Instantly Ian was to his feet, running out of the kitchen only to sprint up the stairs to his bedroom. Sounds of a struggle became louder the closer he got to his door. Ceana screamed, a high-pitched, blood-curdling sound of terror.

"Ceana!" Ian yelled, kicking open his door. Claws grew from the tips of his fingers and his fangs lengthened. He was ready to fight. His eyes darted to the bed and he stopped cold. "Meghan? What are you doing here?"

"I came to apologize for last night, but you didn't answer your door when I knocked and then I heard a scream..." Meghan stood next to Ceana, who was still out of it, thrashing and moaning in her nightmarish sleep about being turned into a mermaid.

Ian went to her and laid a hand on her head. Instantly, she stopped moving and settled once more.

"Meghan?" James and Roark repeated at the same time from the door.

"Shh, let's get out of here," Ian ordered. He stroked back Ceana's hair gently only to stop as he felt Meghan's eyes burning into him. Glancing at her, he watched her quickly hide her jealousy with a vacant smile. "She needs sleep."

Striding out of the room, he didn't wait to see if Meghan followed.

Wonderful! Just grand! Meghan's anger and jealousy is the last thing I need to deal with right now. The woman will probably spread the news of Ceana's ramblings to the whole clan by nightfall.

And no doubt she'll expand upon it as well, James' voice invaded.

Ian sighed. He'd forgotten to guard the thoughts from his brothers. Kicking James out of his head, he led the way down the stairs, making sure Meghan followed them. She did, but a pout was on her full lips and she didn't look too pleased.

"Now's not a good time, Meghan," Ian said, just wanting the woman gone.

"But..." She glanced up the stairs. Then, frowning, she glared at Ian.

"Ah, well, look at that. I left my beer in the kitchen," Roark said, grabbing James and hauling him to the other room to give Ian privacy.

Ian kept his eyes trained on Meghan. "I never promised you anything. In fact, I believe I remember telling you that nothing would come of us. I've only been brutally honest with you. If you didn't listen, that is your own doing. Not mine."

"That was fifty years ago!" she exclaimed. "So, what? You've just been using me all these years? And now you think you can just toss me aside because you find some little bimbo piece of driftwood in the ocean? You dare to bring her here and fuck her?"

"This is my house and I'll fuck whoever I want in it. Don't pretend to be the victim. You have used my position within the clan to your advantage. I know that you require some of the others to do you favors. I know that you've threatened to rip other women's throats out of their necks if they talked to me again. I've tolerated your insolence and your highhandedness because you were my lover. But no more. It's over, Meghan. I should have stopped you when I first heard the rumors decades ago. You will never be queen. And so help me, if you act in such a way again, I will have you brought up on charges and tried by the whole clan."

"How dare you!" she gasped. "You can't discard me like a piece of trash!"

"Meghan, please, don't do this. We had some good times and you've enjoyed them as much as I have. Go, find a young lycan with virile blood and settle down."

MICHELLE M. PILLOW

Meghan screeched at the top of her lungs, screaming at him as she stormed for the front door. She flung it open behind her and ran out, cursing him the whole way. Ian took a deep breath.

"That went well," Roark said from the doorway.

Ian turned, both brothers were standing there, obviously having listened.

"She's not done," James warned.

"Yes, she is," Ian assured him.

"*Ahh!*"

This time the scream was from Ceana upstairs. Ian growled, angry at Meghan for her tirade. It only woke Ceana up. He ran back up the stairs, motioning his brothers to stay back.

10

Ceana took several deep breaths as she sat on the bed. She ached all over, her chest was sore and her throat scratchy. She was alive and was very much human. Could it be the curse was over?

Closing her eyes, she remembered with renewed clarity the witch's curse. As with all curses, there was always a way to end them. Urbana had thought of that though, and put her own ending on it—a most impossible one. Or so Ceana thought.

By the formidable power of the Cancerian Crab, I condemn you... The sea will be your home and the full moon your only respite.

The first part was simple. The sea had been her home and she'd been forced to land for her "respite" each full moon for centuries. In fact, there were a few

75

times when she had to hold on to boats when crossing too much territory in the ocean, or even hide out on their decks, huddled in a corner and praying the men didn't see her. A naked woman in the middle of nowhere would have been a tempting treat for pirates.

But the second part?

Only one can break this curse. One so rare you should never find him. You must find the love from one of land, born under the sign of Cancer, born of the night, ruled by the moon. Only he can break this spell. Only his pure love can set you free.

Was Ian the one? He was from the land. But that was idiotic really. Like she'd really find love with a fish. And as a wolf man, was he ruled by the moon? Born of the night? Was he born under the Cancer sign?

Did he love her? Pure love?

Ceana took a deep breath, the thoughts whirling in her head. They became overbearing. And then, calmness.

Ian opened the door seconds after the feelings overwhelmed her.

"When were you born?" she asked him.

He closed the door and stepped toward the bed. His eyes darted down and Ceana realized she was naked. She was so used to being so that she didn't really think about it. Pulling the covers up to get his hot gaze off her breasts, she repeated, "When were you born?"

"It is you, isn't it? But how?" He stepped closer. "Did you get pulled through some time portal? Are you reborn? I don't understand. You should be dead."

"You know about me?" she gasped. "No, it's the curse. I've been in the ocean, waiting for you. It is you, isn't it? The one to break the curse? When were you born?"

"You don't really remember, do you?" he asked, looking sad. "I was drawn to the water and almost drowned, you saved my life."

"It happened yesterday," she said, feeling like they were having two different conversations, neither of them getting the answers they sought.

"No, yesterday was the second time. It happened long ago, centuries in fact. I looked for you but you disappeared."

Ceana frowned. If they'd crossed paths before then why was the curse ending now. Did he love her now and not then?

"I nearly went mad looking for you," Ian continued.

She shook her head. "I rescued many over the

centuries, almost every full moon. The call you felt to the ocean is the call they all feel. You cannot be him. You don't love me, do you? But, I don't understand. How is the curse broken? If you don't truly love me then how did it end? Tell me, please, when were you born? What sign?"

"Cancer," he answered. "I was born a Cancer."

"And of the night?" she asked. "Being wolf, would you say you are of the night? Born of the moon?"

"The full moon controls me—"

"And the night?" Ceana rushed, excited.

"Yes, you could say that."

"Then you are the one. You freed me from my curse. It has to be you. Otherwise how...?" She looked at her hands. "I was a mermaid. I was trapped in the water. The witch cursed me and she said only one could free me. You're him, Ian. You freed me."

"I don't know about that," he said, looking uncomfortable by her words.

"You do believe me, don't you, Ian?" A loud rumbling gurgled in her stomach and she looked down, startled by the sound.

He frowned. "You're getting worked up. Come on, let's get you cleaned up and fed. You've had a rough morning."

Ceana smiled at him, remembering the night. "We had a wonderful night, though, didn't we?"

He cleared his throat. "Yes, it was fun."

Fun? Sex like that and all he could say was fun?

Coming off the bed, she stood naked before him. His eyes drifted down over her naked body, to the thatch of curls guarding her pussy. A low sound came from the back of his throat as he tore his gaze away. Turning toward a tall piece of furniture, he pulled open a door. Grabbing a shirt from within, he handed it back to her without looking. Ceana frowned and took it. She held it on her upturned hand, keeping it neatly folded.

"You need a shower," he said. "Come on."

Ceana followed him, carrying the shirt as he led her from the room. Curious, she looked all around. She didn't remember houses looking like this, with smooth walls and odd colors. His room had been light, but the hall had blue trim at the ceiling.

"Do all houses look like this nowadays?" she asked.

"No."

There was something in his flat tone that kept her from asking any more. The floors changed from wood to stone as he brought her to a smaller room.

Sitting on a white chair, she stiffened and jumped up.

"It's cold!"

He frowned, looking where she pointed. Sounding confused, he said, "It's a toilet."

"The toilet is a cold chair," she told him, nodding.

"Ah, I'll explain it to you later," he said. Turning to an even smaller room with wavy clear walls, he reached in. Suddenly, water squirted out of the top of it. Ceana screamed, grabbing her arms and looking down at her legs. The shirt dropped to the floor.

"Holy Balls! What?"

"Ah." Ceana looked helplessly at the shower.

"It's just water. Get in. Soap's here," he paused, lifting a green container before pointing. "There's shampoo, conditioner and over here are fresh towels. Yell if you need anything, I'll wait outside. And make sure you shut the door so it doesn't leak through the ceiling downstairs."

Ian hurried and left. She tilted her head, staring after him. He was walking stiffly. Was he aroused? It was too hard to tell.

Ceana slowly crept to the water. She stuck her shaking hand in to see if a fin would grow. When it didn't, she braved the second hand.

"Everything all right in there?" Ian called.

"Ah, yes!" Stepping inside, she closed the door behind her. She stood tense for several moments. The warm water felt good but it took her a moment to relax. When the fresh water splashed into her mouth and she didn't get gills, she finally moved to take the soap. Luckily, the whole speaking the local language thing was also applicable to reading and she was able to understand the directions on what to do with the stuff.

11

AFTER HER SHOWER, Ceana grabbed the towel Ian indicated she was to use and dried off. Placing the towel on the rack, she was startled to see movement out of the corner of her eye. It took a second to register, but the movement was her reflection. Staring at herself in fascination, she touched the image. Her skin was pale and she looked as young as the day the curse started. Tears glistened in her eyes—they were the same eyes her brother had. She wondered what had happened to him. Did he marry? Have kids? Lead a happy life?

It was so long ago, there was surely no way of knowing. Touching her hair, she picked up a long piece. It was messy and smelled strange, almost herbal, from the rinses Ian gave her to use. Ceana dropped the lock and turned to go. Detecting a strange scar on her neck, she stopped and leaned forward. She touched it and realized it wasn't a scar. It was the trace of a gill. Panicked, she looked at her arms. Two thin lines had appeared where the fins would come out.

Biting her lip, she shook her head and whispered, "No."

"No, what?" Ian called from the other side of the door.

Frowning, she whispered really softly. "Can you hear me?"

"Well, of course I can hear you." He sounded irritated with her.

"I'm done," Ceana said. She opened the bathroom door and stepped out, completely naked.

"I've got food downstairs ready for you if you're..." Ian glanced up from where he sat on the floor. His back was against the wall and his voice stopped the moment his gaze landed on her breasts. "Ah."

"Mmm, thank you." Ceana stepped over his legs and walked down the stairs.

"Oh, a-ah," Ian stuttered. She heard him standing up as she went down. "No, stop!"

She paused, turning to him.

"You're..." he paused and motioned at her.

Ceana glanced down. Oh, she was naked again. Giving him a sheepish smile, she shrugged, "I forget, it's been awhile since I've had clothes. I don't own any."

"Hey, Ian, is this hot sauce brand any good? I want to put it into James' coffee before he comes bac —k me into a wall and call me big daddy! *Helllo*, darling."

Ceana smiled at the man at the bottom of the stairs as he let loose a low whistle. "Hello. Are you related to Ian? You look like him."

"Roark!" Ian bellowed, stomping down the stairs. He grabbed her arm and jerked her behind his back, blocking her from view. "Get out of this house now."

"I might look like him on the outside, but downstairs I'm much bigger," Roark assured her, winking impudently.

Ceana giggled.

"Roark! Now!" Ian bellowed. Roark, whistling once more, sauntered out of sight. Only when a loud thud sounded did Ian turn around to look at her. His eyes were golden and his fangs had lengthened in his mouth. Growling, he took an aggressive step up, forcing her to walk back as he moved forward.

"He seems friendly," Ceana offered weakly. "Are you close?"

"Not so close as to share," Ian answered. The beast was even in his gravelly voice.

Ceana tried to smile, but Ian looked too mad. Confused, she asked, "You don't trust him with your...things?"

At her words, his eyes yellowed, giving away the danger of his shift. "You will not fuck my brothers."

Ceana gasped. "I didn't... Ah, you...?"

"Listen well, Ceana," he demanded roughly before she could gather her thoughts to even respond. "You will fuck no other males! And you will wear clothing around any other male. Do you understand me? You are mine and you will not saunter around here naked unless only you and I are home. And you will not flirt with Roark! Do you understand me?"

He was breathing hard and wasn't making any sense, but the gist of his message was very clear.

"Home?" she repeated, saying the only thing she could think of after his tirade. "My home is here? With you?"

The question took him aback and he stopped his aggressive pursuit of her. "Only until we figure out what to do with you."

"What to do with me?" she repeated, looking

down at her arms. The lines were gone, but the memory that they'd started to surface wasn't. What if the fins came back for good? Now that she was out of the water, she didn't want to go back.

"I just meant—"

"No, it's fine," she assured him. But it wasn't fine.

"Ceana? What is it?"

"You never answered me. Do you believe me about the sea witch? About me being cursed?" Ceana touched his face.

"I should say no," he answered. "But I want to believe you. I just don't think I'm the one to have broken any curse."

Unable to stop herself, Ceana grabbed him and kissed him, drinking in the sweet taste of his mouth as she ravished him with her tongue. She was determined to show him that he felt something for her. He had to. How else would she be standing here now?

"Ian? Roark?" a voice called.

Ian pulled back and gasped. Keeping hold of his face, she stared into his eyes. "Get out of my house, James! Now!"

"Right, then!" James answered. "Call you later!"

Ceana grinned and thrust her body against him. The thrill of him was in her blood. He growled in the back of his throat, lifting her up so her legs were forced around his hips. His hard cock pressed into her through his clothing and she squirmed against him in longing. Ian walked her rest of the way up the stairs. Without stopping, he kept kissing her as he carried her to his bedroom. Pleasure exploded over her nipples and clit, racking her body in continual waves, heating her until she forgot all her questions.

Ian's hands were all over her body. He massaged her lower back, her hips, dipping his hands over her ass and gripping it tightly. Urgently, she tried to touch him everywhere at once. His lips trailed over her neck, causing her to shiver as he nibbled her ear.

When he let her legs drop to the floor, she looked into his eyes. They were golden with an eternal fire. Intently, he reached for her breasts, lightly stroking her nipples into erect points. Her pussy ached to be filled, to have his stiff cock thrusting into her once more, stretching her wide as she knew he would.

Ian pulled his shirt over his head and tossed it aside, revealing his muscled chest. Breathing heavily, she watched him undress for her. There was only a foot of space between them, but she held back in anticipation. She watched his hands go to his waist, as he worked his pants free. The material slid to the floor, unveiling his thick erection. Now free, his cock seemed to grow impossibly bigger, standing tall from the soft bed of hair between his thighs. Veins threaded over the sides of it, leading her eyes to the impossibly thick tip of his powerful cock head moist with pre-cum. She licked her lips, automatically wanting to taste him, touch him, fuck him hard and long. Her pussy released a torrent of cream in eager anticipation.

Reaching for him, she ran her hands over his chest. Ian took a deep breath, as if he could smell her body's desire for him. She ran her hands down his flat stomach to his cock, only to grab the turgid shaft firmly in her palms. Ian threw back his head and groaned. Using both hands, she pumped her fists over his penis several times.

Ian jerked her against his body once more. She gasped, engulfed within the smell of him, the seductive fragrance of his flesh. Her loins tightened in anticipation. He shifted his hips until his cock wedged along her soaked sex, hot and so very alive.

Ceana shivered and moaned. Cream practically dripped from her thighs, making her squirm. Ian took a step forward, pushing her toward the bed. His nostrils flared and a low growl sounded in the back of his throat. Kissing her neck, he ran his hot tongue over her pulse. He pushed her onto the bed, falling with her to the soft mattress. She parted her legs, opening herself to him in offering as he settled between her hips.

Ian took his time exploring her front, licking and probing with a tender fierceness, before swiftly flipping her over onto her stomach. Ceana gripped the mattress as his hands glided over her flesh, kneading her ass, spreading her cheeks. The texture of his palms changed, becoming rougher, and she knew he was starting to shift. He trailed light kisses down her spine, only to follow the caress with the erotic press of his nails. When his kisses reached the back of her thighs, he slipped a finger between her legs and found the slick folds guarding her sex. She squirmed, trying to push back on his hand. Ian chuckled, a low, dominant sound.

"You smell so good," he said, his tone husky. "And your taste... *Mmmm!*"

Ian pulled his hand away, and she could hear the loud sounds of his mouth sucking her cream from it. Grabbing her hips, he hauled her to her hands and knees.

"Look at this sweet ass of yours," he growled. "I must have been tired from our ordeal in the water to not have fucked it last night."

His cock probed her from behind and she tensed, thinking he meant to spear her anus with it. Instead, he slipped it along her slit, spreading her pussy wide and pressing along her opening so just the thick tip of him entered her.

"Ah, yeah, that's it, baby." Ian stroked her clit in small circles as he eased his cock in and out in shallow thrusts. "Get me nice and wet. Holy Balls, you feel good. When I'm done with you no lycan will dare touch what is mine."

Ceana felt hope at his words. He wasn't like other men. Others had declared their love, making her think it was the spell they were under. Ian said nothing about his feelings. But when he looked at her, there was something in his eyes. And the fact that she wasn't in the ocean right now had to mean something.

Slowly, he pressed forward, as if savoring the moment. When he hit deep, he pulled out only to ease in again. His finger slipped in her body's moisture only to come around to the tight rosette of her ass. Probing her, he sighed heavily, and said, "You're so tight, this might hurt. Try to relax."

All she could do was moan in response. He drew his cock up between her cheeks and she tensed as she waited for that first press. His thick mass stretched her open, hitting all the sensitive nerve endings at once. She'd never felt anything like it.

Ian kept going. He was so thick, fitted so tight, it was like he was molding her body to him. Then, with a final thrust, he seated his cock deep into her ass. Ceana cried out at the intense pleasure-pain of the moment. It felt too good, like nothing she'd ever done before.

With a dominant roar, Ian grabbed her roughly by the hips and began riding her from behind, trapping her to him. Ceana dug her hands into the mattress, letting him have his way with her. She wanted this moment, loved the all-conquering feel of his claim on her.

"Argh!" he cried, pumping faster.

Ceana tensed, unable to make a sound as her orgasm hit her. He kept going, his primal grunts echoing around her. His nails raked her skin before his hands tightened on her hips. When he came, shooting his seed inside her, she felt energy pulse from where they were joined, spreading over her entire length, filling her with warmth and intense pleasure. Her limbs numbed and her eyesight dimmed. She'd never felt anything like it.

Ian slowly withdrew, only to fall down on the bed beside her. Ceana curled next to him. He was breathing hard, the harsh sound warring with the thud of her heartbeat in her ears.

❧

IAN COULDN'T BELIEVE how wonderful he felt in the aftermath of their lovemaking. Every fiber in his being was calm, as if her presence centered him. She was everything he'd ever wanted. Odd, since he'd just met her. But, his kind acted on instinct and he trusted his. The only problem was, would his people? Would the O'Connell Clan agree with his choice? Or would they, like James, think she was crazy?

Words welled within him and he wanted to tell her how he felt. He'd been trying to swallow them back, trying to keep from saying anything he'd later regret. Ian didn't believe in lying or giving a word he couldn't keep. So instead, he thought it, hoping that his tongue would be satisfied with that much and hold back a little longer.

I love you, Ceana. I don't know how or why, but I love you.

There, he'd thought it. No need to say it aloud. Then why did the urge only grow stronger, as did his renewing desire for her?

"Mmm," she moaned softly, as if she'd heard him.

"Come to the shower with me," he said, running a hand over the small of her back. "We should clean off."

Ceana stiffened. "But, I, ah, already showered."

"Mmm, baby, I know you feel tired. Come on, I promise I'll make it worth it."

Ceana arched a brow, looking at him. There was hesitance there. He'd gotten mixed signals from her. The night before, she told him not to fall in love with her. But early today, she asked him if he did love her, as if she wanted him to.

Or was he reading too much into it? It's not like he'd done this kind of thing before. He'd never really been in love. His father always claimed that it hit hard, like a kick to the chest.

You've waited a long time for her. This is the one, the thoughts whispered in his head.

"What are you thinking?" she whispered, her stormy gaze wide.

Grinning, Ian swept her into his arms and carried her out of the bedroom. Her head rested against his shoulder. Back in the bathroom, he turned the warm water on and, as the steady stream pelted them, he couldn't resist making love to her again—this time slower as he held her up against the wall.

12

CEANA PULLED the robe Ian lent her to wear closer to her body. This wasn't good. After she'd made love with Ian in the shower, the fins had started to come back, this time poking through the skin. Her legs had also started to shimmer with the look of scales, though they did not mold together to form a fin.

She's artfully managed to hide them from him, not sure if showing him would scare him or drive him away. At this rate though, how much time did she really have? Did something in Ian keep her from transforming back as quickly? Did something happen at the beach that made her human longer?

Ceana couldn't figure it out. If some element had been different with Ian, and if it wasn't to break the curse, than she would surely go mad trying to discover what had happened. Taking a deep breath, she looked down at the plate in front of her. The crab was cooked, but she couldn't bring herself to take a bite.

"You don't like crab?" Ian asked, frowning at her.

"I..." Ceana looked at the fried strips and then back up. "I'm not allowed to eat it."

"What are you allowed to eat?"

"Raw fish."

"Sushi?"

"Ah, no, just raw fish." She pushed the plate away. "Though, to tell the truth, nothing from the sea sounds very appetizing right now."

Ian chuckled lightly, but didn't elaborate at what he thought was funny. "Would you prefer your crab raw?"

"I can't eat crab. At all. The sea witch used its power to curse me. I..." She looked helplessly at him. "I just can't."

"All right. I'll find something else." He stood and began the process of opening drawers and rummaging through cabinets.

"You don't want to know about the curse?" she asked. "Why don't you ask me about it? Anyone else would want to know."

"Okay, how were you cursed?"

"I saved my brother from drowning. Well, actually, he'd been entranced by the sea witch. She was going to marry him and then drown him. I followed him one night and saw what he couldn't. To him she was just a beautiful young maiden and he was in love with her. So I drugged him and tied him up. I went to the sea witch to tell her to leave my brother alone. And she, in her anger, cursed me for all eternity because of it."

"And you believe I have broken this curse?" Ian asked.

"I don't know." Slowly, she stood. She couldn't bear not being honest with him. Crossing to the sink, she turned on the water and pulled up the robe sleeve. She put her arm under water, watching as a fin protruded from beneath her skin. It poked out a little more, but not all the way.

Ian dropped a container and she jolted in surprise at the loud crash. When she looked at him, he was staring at her arm.

"So it really is true," he whispered.

"Yes, it's true. I thought you broke the curse, but now I don't know. Maybe you just delayed it for a day. I can feel myself changing back. My guess is by nightfall, at this rate, I'll be back in the ocean. Sunset would be a fitting time, wouldn't it? Perhaps the sea witch has thought of other ways to torment me."

"And if we keep you from water?"

"I don't think it will matter," Ceana sighed. "If I don't get to water and I change back, then I'll die."

"My father," Ian said, thoughtfully.

"Your father?" she asked, not following what he meant.

"My father is king of the O'Connell Clan. If anyone knows about this kind of thing, surely it would be him. He'll be at the beach tonight. Near the same place we were at. The clan is gathering there. It's more of a reunion than anything, but..." Ian's voice trailed off. He stepped over the dropped container to come to her side. "Will you come with me?"

"Yes." Ceana nodded. What else could she do?

"You'll need something to wear," Ian said. "Come on. We'll get you something at the local market to eat and then we'll find you something to wear."

"And tonight, if your father can't help us?" she asked.

"Then tonight..." He took a deep breath and touched her cheek. "Then I guess you swim out of my life."

13

CEANA LOOKED AT THE SAND, scooping it up between her naked toes. The sound of the ocean hitting upon the shore called to her, urging her toward it. The rhythmic sound was soothing yet lonely. She didn't dare go in the water. If she got wet, she was afraid of what might happen. She might not stay human.

It occurred to her that, if she did become a mermaid, she could always come to shore on the full moons to Ian. Would he agree to that? Or would he grow bored with his mermaid lover? Get tired of waiting for a full moon? Was it fair to even ask it of him? If other men had gone mad after one night with her, then what would several do? And if not he, than surely she would be driven into insanity. There were some nights, as she sat alone in her sunken ship, staring at a random portrait faded by ocean water that she was close to madness already.

And what happened when he did die? He might be lycan, but that didn't make him immortal. Ian had said as much himself while they were shopping for the floral dress she now wore. Large blue-gray flowers contrasted with the cream background. Buttons ran all the way down the front stopping only a few inches from the knee-length hem. The short sleeves capped her shoulders and the neckline scooped open to show off her collarbones, but no cleavage.

Feeling a hand against the small of her back, she glanced up at Ian. His smile was strained as he nodded down to where his clan gathered. After having been alone for so long, she wasn't sure she could face the crowd, especially one filled with Ian's family members.

"Ready?" he asked.

His face was strained and he didn't look very happy about the prospect of her being introduced. Was he changing his mind? The day had been fun. They'd walked along some of the seaside shops, holding hands and enjoying the fine, sunny weather. He'd even led her into a hidden corner off the main walk and proceeded to make love to her against the wall.

When she didn't answer, he gave her a gentle shove down toward where the bonfires lit up the beach. The sun was lowering in the sky, but had yet to touch the horizon. Lycans were gathered, sitting around the fires. Some laughed, others tuned instruments, strumming absent notes as they talked.

Seeing an older man who looked like Ian, she tried to smile. It was obviously his father. The man raised a brow when he looked at her before turning to Ian.

"Son," the man said, grinning widely, as he unwittingly confirmed his relationship to Ian. "So it is true. You found a mermaid."

Ian stopped and looked at Ceana. His mouth opened, but no sound came out as his father joined them.

"Meghan found me earlier and told me you'd pulled a young lady from the sea." The man turned to her. "And you must be the mermaid."

"Ceana," she said.

"Wait, how do...?" Ian asked, clearly confused.

"Didn't Meghan find you? She said you knew she was talking to me and that you'd asked her to track me down. You two have been together for so long, I just assumed that..." Suddenly, the man stopped and looked at her, sniffing. "Ian? You marked this one? The mermaid?"

Ceana studied Ian, waiting to see what he would say.

"No, I'm not with Meghan and I sure as hell didn't send her to talk to you." He glanced around. "I'll get to the bottom of this. Where is she?"

"I haven't seen her since early afternoon, right after lunch," Ian's father said. "Is this something the family needs to be concerned about?"

"I told her she would never be my wife. She wasn't happy about it. After she left my house this morning, she must have gone to find you. What exactly did you tell her?"

"Only that when I was younger I knew of a sea witch who had the power to condemn young women to the sea. And if you were one of these mermaids, she wouldn't be too happy about you getting out of the water." The lycan king studied her. "I never thought I'd live to see one."

"Urbana," Ceana said softly.

"Yes, that's what she was called," the king said. "So, is it true? You're one of her cursed?"

Ceana nodded.

"And can I assume by your mark on her, Ian, that

you are going to break her curse and free the mermaid?" The king looked hopeful.

"I don't know how," said Ceana.

"What was the curse?" the king asked.

"To live in the ocean, except during full moons until one came to break the curse." She glanced at Ian. "That my only hope is to find the one who can break the curse—a man from land, born under the right sign and of the moon. Also, he must be born of the night."

"What sign?" the king asked.

"Cancer. It was by the power of the Cancerian Crab that it happened."

"Genius," the king whispered. "So specific it would be hard to fulfill."

"Ah..." Ceana looked helplessly at Ian.

"Oh, sorry, love," he said. "I didn't mean anything by it." Turning to his son, the king added, "But it really is a precise curse. Not many people would know what to look for."

"And you know what to look for?" Ceana asked, trying not to sound too eager, even as her heart leapt around in her chest."

"It's Ian, all right." The king looked at his son. "Born of Cancer and the night. He's from land and ruled by the moon as all lycans are."

"There's one more thing," Ceana continued softly. "His love must be pure."

"Ah, she must have really been mad at you to be so specific in her anger." The king patted her arm. "So, I guess there's really only one question then."

Ian didn't speak. He looked stunned.

"I'm changing back," Ceana said. "Whenever I touch water I grow partial fins. I fear I don't have much more time on land."

"I'd imagine that is to be expected," the king nodded thoughtfully. "In the old days, the purest of loves were expressed when two people defied all odds and were married. Since marriages, especially with humans, were arranged, undoubtedly that is how Urbana's curse played out. Though times have changed, the curse will have not. Whether that is what she intended or not, I have no way of knowing. But I imagine that is what has happened. Magic is a very tricky thing to get exact. In all honesty, practitioners of it can never be sure of the exact results. I myself have only dabbled, but that was a long time ago."

"I just don't get what use Meghan would have with this information," Ian said. His father shrugged. Ceana noticed how Ian avoided the topic of marriage completely. Could she really blame him? He hardly knew her.

"You'll have to ask her," the king answered. "She told me she was coming tonight." Pausing, he sniffed the air. "Ah, it looks like she just arrived."

"She lied to you about me sending her to inquire," Ian said.

"Yes, and I suppose she'll be punished for using your name in such a way and for lying to me." The king patted Ian's shoulder. "Though, truth be told, you have allowed her certain liberties over the years. Perhaps she thought it was her right."

"I made myself clear to her," Ian said. "I never lied about my feelings."

Ceana didn't like the sound of this Meghan. Mainly, because she was jealous of the woman. Meghan evidently had known Ian for a long time and quite intimately.

"Well, perhaps you should go ask her," the king said, motioning to where the beach rose to a small incline. They all turned. On the hill a woman was outlined in orange, as if the sun put its personal spotlight on her.

"I will," he said.

Ian took Ceana's arm and walked to where Meghan seemed to be standing in wait for them.

Music started and several of the lycans called out to Ian. He ignored them and they let him be. As they neared the woman, Ceana shivered. She had long, jet-black hair and dark eyes that glinted with a dangerous gold.

Meghan turned her back on them and walked away from the bonfires. Ian didn't stop in his progress. Ceana glanced back to the king. He was grinning at her. When their eyes met, he winked, raising his mug of beer before turning to talk to a nearby group of lycan men.

"Meghan!" Ian ordered when they were out of sight of the bonfires.

"Come, Ian, I have something to show you," the woman answered, her voice as sugary as warm honey. Ceana also had the distinct impression that the woman could also be venomous if she so chose.

"Meghan, stop!" he ordered.

She did, turning to him with a look of impatience. "Yes, darling?"

Darling? Ceana wanted to kick the woman. Unfortunately, she didn't know how to fight.

"You have some explaining to do. By what right do you interfere in this matter?" he demanded.

"Oh," Meghan pouted. "You don't trust me?"

"Meghan," he warned, drawing out the sound of

her name. He let go of Ceana's arm and she stepped back, watching the two closely. She tried to see past her own jealousy to what was really happening.

"I just wanted to protect you, darling," she purred. "We don't know anything about this woman. She could mean you harm. I mean, you just picked the slut up last night and already she's in your home?" Meghan clicked her tongue and glanced disdainfully in her direction, but otherwise did not acknowledge she was there. "Not very smart, Ian."

"Who I sleep with is none of your concern." Ian placed his hands on his hips.

"For your information, I went to your father to protect you and because I was worried about you. I've known you for a long time and suddenly, you ditch me and throw me on my ass for a piece of shark bait? I don't think so, buddy. Besides, my assumptions were right. After I talked to your father, I did some more research. The reason you dumped me on my ass was because she made you do it. She's a mermaid. She calls men to their deaths in the sea. That's what her kind does and then she feeds off their dead, bloated flesh."

"I would never," Ceana began.

"What else would you say, flesh eater?" Meghan spat.

"She saved me," Ian argued. Still, when he turned to look at her, Ceana saw distrust in his eyes. "She pulled me out of the water. Twice."

"To fuck you no doubt," Meghan spat. "Ian, why would I lie to you about this? You know I've only ever cared about you."

"My title," Ian corrected.

"Damn it, Ian! You're supposed to eat fish, not fuck it!" Meghan glared at Ceana. "And you. I know what you are. I know what you want. Your mistress, the sea witch told me all about you."

"Urbana?" Ceana paled, involuntarily backing away from the shoreline. "She's here?"

"And she's not happy to have you out of the ocean," Meghan spat. "What did she tell you, Ian? That she was a victim of the sea witch? She's not a victim. She's being punished for drowning her brother in cold blood."

"What?" Ceana shook her head. "No. No, that's not what happened. I didn't hurt Kerrigan. I... Ian?"

"Ah, so convincing, isn't she? But not all of us are fooled by the conniving bitch." Meghan pointed back to the sea. "If you don't believe me, go ask the witch yourself. Urbana will show you everything."

"Ceana?" Ian asked.

It took her a moment to look at him. There was

confusion in his tone and she knew he had doubts about her.

"Ian, I already told you. She can't be trusted." Meghan went to him, reaching for his arm.

He jerked away from her. "This changes nothing, Meghan. You are still in trouble for lying to the king. Let us hope, for your sake, you are not lying to me now." He stepped past her toward the shore. "Come, Ceana. We'll find out who is telling the truth in this. Meghan. Call your friend."

"No," Ceana pleaded. "You don't know what you're up against. Ian, please. Don't do this. I... I'm scared of her. Please. Don't take me to the ocean."

He stopped, his expression softening. "Ceana, baby, I know you're scared. I'm scared too. Not of the witch, but of what I feel for you right now. I have to know that it's not a trick. I have to know that I haven't been under a spell. And if there is a curse, I need to see Urbana. If there is a way to break it, I would know how. She might be the only one who truly knows."

Ceana took a deep breath and nodded. What else could she say? He was right. And the hint that he might care deeply for her made her legs feel stronger. She walked with him toward the water. Meghan glared openly at her, looking ready to shift and tear Ceana's eyes out.

As they neared the shore, Ceana suddenly stopped. Her heart quickened and the pull to the ocean became unbearable. Gasping, her feet started to slide forward in the sand. Her arms flailed and she screamed.

"Ceana!" Ian yelled, reaching out to grab her. He missed as her body gained momentum.

The sand heated beneath her feet. Throwing her body, she landed on the ground and began reaching for pieces of driftwood—anything that would keep her from the water. The wood only slid with her. Nothing helped. Suddenly, a loud roar sounded and she looked up to see Ian running toward her. His body shifted and dark brown fur grew over his flesh. His eyes narrowed and his body sped through the night with ease to reach her. Just as her feet dipped into the cold ocean water, he reached her. She grabbed at his front paw and he pulled her back.

"Leave her, lycan. She is mine!" The angry words resounded over the beach, punctuated by the violent crash of waves toward the shore. Suddenly, silvery light flashed as the witch appeared to join her voice. Ceana looked at the water, seeing the horrible, watery shape growing up from the surface. Two fat

CALL OF THE SEA

eels swam inside her chest, their bodies ripping the surface of her skin as they poked through.

The fur beneath her hand disappeared, to be replaced by flesh. She looked up. Her eyes meeting Ian's dark ones.

"Run, Ian," Ceana yelled, as the waves swept up and touched her feet. He didn't listen as he tried to drag her away. "Don't let the water touch you! It's too late for me. She owns my soul. But you can save yourself."

"Meghan!" Ian roared. "For the love of the lycan clan, help me pull her!"

Meghan's sharp laughter rang out. "See what you get, Ian, for messing with me! That bitch will never have you. You are such a fool. And now, you will live with the knowledge that you brought her here, to the shore. It was your doubt that sent her back to the ocean."

Ian pulled Ceana violently behind him.

"No!" the sea witch screeched as Ceana's body jerked loose from the water.

From the corner of her eye, Ceana saw Meghan back away. Suddenly, the treacherous woman turned, running from them.

"Ian!" Ceana pointed after Meghan.

Ian looked but didn't appear too concerned about

111

the woman's escape. "Don't worry about her. She might run now, but my brother will find her. Roark hunts our lawbreakers for a living. He'll like bringing her in."

"Ian, you should go. Please. Save yourself."

"Marry me!" Ian yelled.

Ceana whipped her head back to look at him. The winds picked up, becoming as violent as the sea. Her breath caught as she looked behind them. The sea witch was approaching fast. Ian tugged her to her feet, urging her to run with him.

"Are you sure, Ian? I don't want you asking because you feel sorry for me."

"Damn it, Ceana! I'm sure. I said it, didn't I? I know it's fast, but I've given the matter all the thought I need. I've never been more sure of anything in my life. I love you. I've loved you since that first night you saved me all those years ago. You were the reason no one else was ever good enough for me. You're the reason I could never give my heart to anyone. I love you, Ceana. Say you'll marry me. Stay with me. Let's break this curse together."

Tears trailed over her face and she nodded. "Yes. Yes. I'll marry you, Ian! I will!"

"No!" Urbana screeched. "You can't!"

"I'm sorry I brought you to the shore," Ian said,

running faster. He was naked and she assumed he must have lost his clothes when his body changed. His strong form moved with perfection over the sand as he sprinted toward where his family gathered around the bonfires. Now was no time to stare at his fine ass, but she couldn't help herself. Even with the sea witch chasing them, she felt protected by Ian. "I just had to know the truth. I didn't mean for you to get sucked into the water like that."

"I know," she answered back.

"Hurry. We'll do it right now. She won't have you. Not again. I won't lose you again."

"Ceana, I call to you, I call you back to your rightful home!" the witch cried.

"Ah!" Ceana's legs cramped. Tears of pain ran over her cheeks as she tripped. "It might be too late."

Her thighs glued themselves together so she couldn't walk. Suddenly, her legs gave out and she felt the tail appearing. She was changing back. Gasping for breath, she felt her neck. The gills were starting to crack through her skin.

"No!" Ian demanded. He swept her up into his arms.

"She is mine!" Urbana screamed.

Ceana looked back in amazement. The woman was on shore, her feet sloshing in the sand as she came after them. Her transparent body shone with the blue of the moonlight. Seaweed wrapped one of her watery legs, winding up her thigh and drifting around as if it were on water. She was formed like a woman, but wore no clothes. Still, there was no human definition to her features, not really. She had a nose and two horrible white eyes that glowed eerily from within.

"Give her to me! It is too late. Too late. She is mine. Give her to me, lycan!" Urbana trudged forward, moving slowly. Her legs jerked up from the sand with each step, as if they took a lot of energy to make.

"You've had her long enough, witch!" Ian cried. Ceana held on, feeling weak, feeling the pull of the sea witch on her body. Her hair drifted up, reaching back behind them toward the witch. As he came to a small hill along the beach, the bonfires were in view. "Father! King Gregor!"

The faint sound of laughter stopped. Ian ran for shore. Ceana was compelled to reach back, though that wasn't what was in her heart to do. In front of them, the lycans stood and several of them began to run toward Ian to help.

"From land to sea," the sea witch cried, "you belong to me!"

She shot out streams of water from her hands, spraying her power like mist from the ocean over those who charged her. Whichever lycan the water landed on, the person instantly dropped to the ground. The victims started to twitch helplessly as they became objects from the sea—starfish, anemones, sand dollars and several types of shells. Ian leapt over his transformed friends. As he neared the fire, he tripped, landing on his knees.

"Father," Ian cried. "I wish to marry this woman. Please may I have your blessing and being king may your blessing also seal my vows!"

"No!" the sea witch hissed, shooting a long stream of water from her hand. It shot over Ceana and Ian and was aimed at the O'Connell king's head.

"So shall it be!" the king yelled. The water suddenly stopped, inches away from his face, and the witch cried out in agony.

Ian leaned over, biting Ceana on the neck. She gasped in surprise as the pain of the touch seared her with a white-hot heat. But soon, the feeling was replaced by pleasure—the pleasure of being completely connected body and soul to her husband. The sensation didn't last long.

Ceana screamed as pain shot over her body. Her tail ripped in half, the sound of it loud and horrible.

Suddenly the frozen water that had come from the sea witch burst above her, sprinkling her and healing her body. Legs grew and the fins fell away to the ground, leaving behind thin scars shaped like a line their wake. Amazed, Ceana stared at the witch. She was glaring with her evil, white eyes. The sea witch screamed, her body bursting into a small but violent spray of droplets just as the stream of water from her hand had.

Ceana couldn't move. She was too stunned. The sea witch was dead.

"My love!" Ian cried, grabbing her to his chest. "It is over. You are safe."

Little explosions of water popped all around them as the lycans turned back to normal. The transformed men and women stumbled around on the sand before finding their footing. Soon, their cries of excitement filled the air.

Ceana was still too stunned to believe that it really was over. She stared at where the witch had dissipated. "But, that woman? Meghan?"

"Don't worry about her. James and Roark will track her down. Her days are numbered." Ian grabbed her face and kissed her. When he pulled away, he announced, "It is done, my love. You are mine."

"We're married!" she gasped, instantly forgetting the witch as she kissed her husband.

"Married?" one of the lycan asked, sounding a little dazed. "Prince Ian has married!"

Shouts sounded. Ceana smiled as two of the men picked up instruments and began to play like nothing had happened. Maybe they were all so old that magic didn't really surprise them anymore.

"My wife!" Ian yelled, hopping to his feet. He pulled her up next to him. She was still a little weak and wobbled until she fell against him.

He grinned like a fool at the cheering crowd around them. Ceana grabbed his face and pulled his mouth quickly to hers. The sounds of the lycans' joy only got louder as she kissed him deeply. When she pulled back, she whispered, "My husband."

Ian grinned, before swaying with her to the beat of the music. Keeping her feet off the ground, he danced with her around the bonfire.

THE END

THE SERIES CONTINUES...

Call of the Untamed
Call of the Lycan Book 2

Roark O'Connell is a lycan on the prowl. For what, he's not always sure. His job within the clan keeps him moving around and boredom often sets in. It's boredom that causes him to make a bet with his brother James to hire an etiquette coach. Expecting an old schoolmarm type, he's blown away to discover the sexiest woman he's ever laid eyes on. The prim and proper Natasha might be there to tame his untamed ways, but he's just the man to fulfill her wildest, most erotic dreams.

Excerpt

Roark O'Connell scratched his ass, yawning as he bumped into one of the many boxes lining his hallway. With a growl, he kicked at the ones partially blocking his bedroom door, causing his toe to get stuck in a cardboard side. The top of the small stack tumbled to the ground. Grumbling, he jerked his foot free, then immediately sweeping it so the boxes were pushed out of his way. Thank goodness they were lightweight and not filled with books. That would have hurt.

The knock again sounded on his front door, reminding him why he was standing upright before noon. It was only his brother James, coming to make sure he got out of bed in time to meet their oldest brother, Ian, who was flying into town with his new wife, Ceana. James was staying at a local hotel. As was his duty as a brother, Roark had offered to let James stay with him, but he'd declined. The last time they'd bunked together the two of them had gotten into a fistfight that would have ended in a funeral had they been humans. It wasn't the first time, and being that they were from a clan of natural-born lycans and were known to have high aggression levels, it wouldn't be the last. Besides, sparring was fun and they could instantly heal any of their own wounds.

I'm coming! he yelled, opening up the telepathic link he had with his brother. The knock sounded again, a short little rap against his door. *I said I'm coming. Hold your fucking horses.*

Leaning against the wall, he rubbed his temples, not really hurrying to answer it. The knock sounded again. Could James not hear him? Or was he purposefully being a jerk?

"You're early, dumbass," Roark growled to himself, knowing James' lycan senses would probably hear the insult. Though he was being grumpy, his brother could hardly take offense at his words.

James was eager to meet with his two brothers before he had to take off on a hunt. His target, Meghan, was a rogue lycan who had betrayed the clan when Ian didn't choose her as a bride. He instead picked Ceana. No doubt, that was what James wanted to consult with them about before going, since their father had appointed him to take the lead on the situation.

Ian's bride had been under a spell, which turned her into a mermaid. Ceana was a sweet woman, a little naïve for his taste, but she was perfect for Ian who had the patience to explain things like how to use a toilet and what stoplights were for. The newly-weds had been house shopping across the country. Roark personally thought it was an excuse for her to see everything she'd missed while in the water.

You shouldn't have brought beer over last night, if you wanted me up this morning, Roark said to him. *Ian and his bride will wait. It's not like we don't have an eternity to spend with them.*

Since becoming free of the centuries-old curse that an evil sea witch had cast upon her, Ceana had developed a fear of the sea. The woman knew more about the ocean than any other human, and she was deathly afraid of it. The O'Connells couldn't blame her for not wanting to step back into the sea. Though even she would admit the fear was unfounded since Ian's love broke the curse and the sea witch was dead —killed by her own arrogance. Being a lycan-mated human she had Ian's long life and health, not to mention the protection of the lycan clan.

Now Ian was bringing her into his area, looking for homes. Roark had moved to Kansas some time ago, and like he did every time he moved, he sent his brothers pictures of the area. Ceana had taken a liking to the landscape. Roark didn't care if they moved nearby, he hardly stayed put long enough to unpack—which was obvious by all the boxes. With modern transportation, it was no longer necessary for the clan to live close together. It wasn't like the old days when they'd have to be able to reach each other on foot in a single night, or be close enough to use telepathy. Just like with speech, the farther apart two lycans were, the harder it was to hear each other's thoughts—though telepathy did reach a lot farther than sound.

Now there were airplanes and cellular phones. In many ways, it had been a blessing. Roark loved his family, but no one could spend an eternity with the same people day after day—well, except if it was a mate. Their father, the king of the lycan clan, had even taken to using webcams for the clan meetings. Technically, Ian was next in line, then James and finally Roark. But, since they were immortal, pending some murderous rampage, it was unlikely that he'd ever rule. Roark was fine with that. He hunted for the clan, just like James, bringing justice to rogue wolves.

Stopping in confusion, Roark looked around. No, he wasn't in Kansas anymore. He'd moved from Kansas to somewhere else. Or did he just move to Kansas? Or did he move from one place in Kansas to another place in Kansas? It was too early and he was too hung-over to think about it. Maybe his family was right, maybe he needed to settle in one place and lay down some roots. Living out of boxes wasn't fun. It was just that he'd never found a reason to stay in any one place too long.

"Shit," he mumbled staring at a box that probably hadn't been unpacked in the last five moves. Blinking and yawning, he tried to kick-start his tired mind. The knock sounded again and he trudged forward. Pulling open the door, he closed his eyes briefly to the bright light of the day and grumbled, "I said I was coming, cocksucker. Now tell me, where the hell did I move to this time? I can't even remember for sure where I am."

"Oh my goodness!"

Roark stiffened in surprise. That didn't sound like James. Suddenly, he realized that James hadn't been answering back as he swore at him through the telepathic link. They must have drunk a lot more than he'd thought the night before. It was odd that he would be this out of it.

Roark focused his eyes on the beauty before him. It sure as hell didn't look like James either. Biting his lip, he moaned without thought, "Damn, baby."

What a way to wake up!

A slender woman with red hair stared at him. She glanced to the side, as if looking at his house. Her hair was pulled high on her head in a bun. Slowly, as she once more turned to look at him, she reached for her sunglasses and pushed them to the top of her head. Roark noted her vibrant blue eyes before letting his gaze travel down. She wore a dress suit—the charcoal gray skirt and jacket over the white silk shirt made for a very formal ensemble—and high-heeled shoes. Her legs were long and he couldn't help but wonder if he was still dreaming. If so, he really didn't want to wake up from this one.

No, dreams don't include hangovers.

"Sir," the woman said, breathing heavily as if she just now found her voice. Her cheeks were flushed and she clearly didn't like the way he'd answered his door. Roark smiled. He could easily make that up to her.

"Mmm." He leaned against the doorframe, putting up his arm to brace his weight.

"Sir," she repeated. Roark's smile widened. Her gaze rounded in mortification as her eyes traveled down. "Ah... *Sir!*"

Roark followed her troubled gaze. Not only had he forgotten that he was naked, he was also obviously aroused from staring at her. Grinning, and completely unapologetic, he winked at the sexy woman. "Morning wood."

"Sir, it's one p.m."

"Really? Hmm, okay, it's afternoon wood."

"Ah." The woman wrinkled her nose. "I'll come back later at a more..."

His smile widened as he gave her a come-hither look. There was something about her that made him want to act the beast. Very rarely did humans have that effect on him. She must have been very special indeed to provoke his body by just the mere sight of her.

In fact, Roark never had such a strong gut reaction to a human. They were a frail people and lycans tended to avoid them as much as possible. An ancient race, the lycans were as old as the humans, growing with them from the very beginning of time, just like all supernatural races. The Church used to condemn the supernaturals as evil pagans, going so far as to hunt and kill them. Times were wilder in the early days, but so it was with all the races—mortal and supernatural. Just as humans no longer roamed the countryside pillaging and wielding swords, his people no longer wildly wielded tooth and fang. Now the lycans hid their existence from the humans. It wasn't difficult, as they were able to smell their mortality instantly on them.

"Appropriate time," she finished weakly. Roark blinked, instantly drawn out of his racing thoughts.

"Why? You're here now." Roark left the door open and turned to go back to his bedroom to find something to put on. He heard her breath catch in her throat as he purposefully flexed his ass as he walked away. "Make yourself at home. I'll just be a moment."

**To find out more about Michelle's books
visit www.MichellePillow.com**

ABOUT MICHELLE M. PILLOW

New York Times & *USA TODAY* Bestselling Author

Michelle loves to travel and try new things, whether it's a paranormal investigation of an old Vaudeville Theatre or climbing Mayan temples in Belize. She believes life is an adventure fueled by copious amounts of coffee.

Newly relocated to the American South, Michelle is involved in various film and documentary projects with her talented director husband. She is mom to a fantastic artist. And she's managed by a dog and cat who make sure she's meeting her deadlines.

For the most part she can be found wearing pajama pants and working in her office. There may or may not be dancing. It's all part of the creative process.

Come say hello! Michelle loves talking with readers on social media!

www.MichellePillow.com

facebook.com/AuthorMichellePillow

twitter.com/michellepillow

instagram.com/michellempillow

bookbub.com/authors/michelle-m-pillow

goodreads.com/Michelle_Pillow

amazon.com/author/michellepillow

youtube.com/michellepillow

pinterest.com/michellepillow

COMPLIMENTARY EXCERPTS

TRY BEFORE YOU BUY!

LOVE POTIONS

BY MICHELLE M. PILLOW

Warlocks MacGregor® Book 1
Contemporary Paranormal Scottish Warlocks

A little magickal mischief never hurt anyone...

Erik MacGregor, from a clan of ancient Scottish warlocks, isn't looking for love. After centuries, it's not even a consideration...until he moves in next door to Lydia Barratt. It's clear that the shy beauty wants nothing to do with him, but he's drawn to her nonetheless and determined to win her over.

Lydia Barratt just wants to be left alone to grow flowers and make lotions in her old Victorian house. The last thing she needs is a demanding Scottish man meddling in her private life. Just because he's gorgeous and totally rocks a kilt doesn't mean she's going to fall for his seductive manner.

But Erik won't give up and just as Lydia let's her guard down, his sister decides to get involved. Her little love potion prank goes terribly wrong, making Lydia the target of his sudden embarrassingly obsessive behavior. They'll have to find a way to pull Erik out of the spell fast when it becomes clear that Lydia has more than a lovesick warlock to worry about. Evil lurks within the shadows and it plans to use Lydia, alive or dead, to take out Erik and his clan for good.

❦

Love Potions Excerpt

"Ly-di-ah! I sit beneath your window, laaaass, singing 'cause I loooove your a—"

"For the love of St. Francis of Assisi, someone call a vet. There is an injured animal screaming in pain outside," Charlotte interrupted the flow of music in ill-humor.

Lydia lifted her forehead from the kitchen table. Her windows and doors were all locked, and yet Erik's endlessly verbose singing penetrated the barrier of glass and wood with ease.

Charlotte held her head and blinked heavily. Her red-rimmed eyes were filled with the all too poignant look of a hangover. She took a seat at the table and laid her head down. Her moan sounded something like, "I'm never moving again."

"You need fluids," Lydia prescribed, getting up to pour unsweetened herbal tea from the pitcher in the fridge. She'd mixed it especially for her friend. It was Gramma Annabelle's hangover recipe of willow bark, peppermint, carrot, and ginger. The old lady always had a fresh supply of it in the house while she was alive. Apparently, being a natural witch also meant in partaking in natural liquors. Annabelle had kept a steady supply of moonshine stashed in the basement. If the concert didn't stop soon she might try to find an old bottle.

"*Ly-di-ah!*"

"Omigod. Kill me," Charlotte moaned. "No. Kill him. Then kill me."

"*Ly-di-ah!*"

Erik had been singing for over an hour. At first, he'd tried to come inside. She'd not invited him and the barrier spell sent him sprawling back into the yard. He didn't seem to mind as he found a seat on some landscaping timbers and began his serenade. The last time she'd asked him to be quiet, he'd gotten louder and overly enthusiastic. In fact, she'd been too scared to pull back the curtains for a clearer look, but she was pretty sure he'd been dancing on her lawn, shaking his kilt.

"Omigod," Charlotte muttered, pushing up and angrily going to a window. Then grimacing, she said, "Is he wearing a tux jacket with his kilt?"

"Don't let him see you," Lydia cried out in a panic. It was too late. The song began with renewed force.

"He's..." Charlotte frowned. "I think it's dancing."

Since the damage was done, Lydia joined Charlotte at the window. Erik grinned. He lifted his arms to the side and kicked his legs, bouncing around the yard like a kid on too much sugar. "Maybe it's a traditional Scottish dance?"

Both women tilted their heads in unison as his kilt kicked up to show his perfectly formed ass.

"He's not wearing..." Charlotte began.

"I know. He doesn't," Lydia answered. Damn, the man had a fine body. Too bad Malina's trick had turned him insane.

To find out more about Michelle's books visit www.MichellePillow.com

REBELLIOUS PRINCE

BY MICHELLE M. PILLOW

Captured by a Dragon-Shifter Series

Cat-shifter Prince Rafe knows that technically he's
supposed to be going to Earth to find a bride, but he
doesn't see the need to rush things. While his dragon-
shifter neighbors appear all too eager to claim their
mates and settle down, he's all for putting that final
moment off and enjoying his little trips through the
portal. Yeah, yeah, eventually he'll have to marry and
set a good example for his people because on his
planet females are rare and they need to have chil-
dren and blah blah blah. But honestly, cat-shifters are
known to embrace their feral side and it would take a
very impressive female to tame his.

Then he sees Jenna Kearney and all bets are off.

PLEASE LEAVE A REVIEW

THANK YOU FOR READING!

Please take a moment to share your thoughts by reviewing this book.

❧

Be sure to check out Michelle's other titles at www.MichellePillow.com